GLASS BEADS

GLASS BEADS

DAWN DUMONT

thistledown press

Thistledown Press Ltd.
410 2nd Avenue North
Saskatoon, Saskatchewan, S7K 2C3
www.thistledownpress.com

Library and Archives Canada Cataloguing in Publication
Dumont, Dawn, 1978–, author
Glass beads / Dawn Dumont.
Short stories.
Issued in print and electronic formats.
ISBN 978-1-77187-126-6 (softcover).–ISBN 978-1-77187-127-3 (HTML).–
ISBN 978-1-77187-128-0 (PDF)

I. Title.
PS8607.U445G53 2017   C813'.6   C2017-901113-8
C2017-901114-6

Cover and book design by Jackie Forrie
Printed and bound in Canada

The writer would like to gratefully acknowledge the funding of the Canada Council for the Arts

Canada Council   Conseil des Arts
for the Arts   du Canada

SASKATCHEWAN
ARTS BOARD

Canadä

Thistledown Press gratefully acknowledges the financial assistance of the Canada Council for the Arts, the Saskatchewan Arts Board, and the Government of Canada for its publishing program.

GLASS BEADS

To Mom and Dad

Contents

Kokum's House

THEY TOLD HER THAT she was no one's baby which would have made her sad except that they had told her that a few times and tears don't come after a while.

This time they didn't want her to have one of the video game controllers and one of them tugged on it in her hand while the other pushed her from behind. She was smaller than them but she could fight better. But if she punched one of them, they would scream until their mom came and then she'd be in real trouble. So she dropped it on the floor with a bang and walked out. One of them called out, "Mom!" So she picked up speed, across the linoleum, through the back door. In a flash. So fast, superfast. The door banged behind her.

She was heading for the treehouse that the girls' dad had built for them. "Our playhouse," they said, meaning not hers. But she could hide there.

"Julie!" Someone yelling behind her. The mom, Doreen. She sounded mad. And Julie didn't want a lickin'. So she kept moving, past the playhouse, into the woods, until she couldn't hear voices anymore.

There were trees everywhere. Because this was the rez. "This is your mother's Indian reserve," the social worker told her. But Julie tried to tell her that her mom didn't live there anymore. She lived in the city and that's where she would be looking for Julie. "Does she know I'm here?" Julie asked and the woman said, "Do you want some candy?" Which Julie took even though it was some kind of hard candy that tasted like Halls and who gives that to kids?

Kokum lived on the reserve. Julie went there once with her mom, it was a day trip and she stood near the door of the house refusing to come all the way in because it was so hot and dark. Kokum sat near the wall in the living room, the wall full of so many pictures, you couldn't even see the paint colour. Kokum kept calling Julie closer. "Come sit on my lap" but Julie didn't do that anymore. When Julie finally came close, because her mom kept bugging her, her grandma pulled her hand into hers and kept squeezing it over and over. And Julie's mom said, "Mom, you're scaring her." Kokum was scary with that tube in her nose and that oxygen tank. But she was nice.

"Can we stay there?" Julie asked her mom as her mom's boyfriend drove them back to the city and her mom said "no, Kokum is sick" and so they were going back to the city. When Julie had bad dreams she would ask her mom again. But the answer was always no.

And when the social worker drove her out to the reserve, Julie thought she was going to Kokum's. But instead she drove her straight to Paul and Doreen's. "They have little girls," she told her. "And you will have lots of fun." Julie didn't ask her about Kokum.

Kokum lives on Stone Man's. Julie knew what the house looked like. *She probably doesn't even know I'm here.* She looked around. There were trees in every direction. Thin birch, naked because it was October. The ground was wet with leaves and Julie could feel her ankles getting wet. Which way was the right way? Not the way she came. Straight ahead looked too cramped with bushes, so she went right because she was right handed. It was nice there in the bushes, the wind was cold but it smelled fresh and sweet. Her feet made a crunchy sound as they squashed the leaves. She could feel her cheeks turning pink. *I am getting my exercise.* On TV, they always said kids didn't get enough exercise.

She saw the deer before she heard them. Two of them standing in the trees in front of her. They looked at her; she looked at them. They returned to eating, deciding that she was okay. She wanted them to stay with her so she stayed still. She broke a piece of branch off and chewed on it, watching them. When her feet started to get cold, she stamped them softly. But not softly enough. The deer looked up at her and then hopped away. "Don't go the way I came," she said. She had seen a deer hanging upside down in Paul's barn. His girls had laughed at her when she didn't want to go in. "We're Indians, stupid," they told her and pushed her inside. Her eyes flitted around like a hummingbird: blood-stained fur, the insides of the deer hanging out and when you looked down at the head, the deer's eyes were open.

Julie watched the deer until they blended into the woods. Maybe these deer would make it. They would be smart and hide in the trees and be okay. Julie's feet were starting to get really cold so she walked faster. The trees were changing, more brush, then a large field of just grain. She walked through that, stopping to break off the grain heads and chew on the stalks, sucking out the nutty marrow. And then there was a house.

There was a swing set in the backyard and Julie thought she could take a break.

What am I going to do with my feet, she wondered as she creaked back and forth on the swing. She could walk forever if it wasn't for her feet. She scrunched her toes together.

And then a voice. "Who are you?"

Julie turned her head. There was a girl standing there, her age. She had on a puffy coat, a hat and mittens, all matching red. She must be rich.

"I'm Angel." It was a name Julie had used before, like when she got caught stealing at the store.

"Nice name." But the girl said it like *I wish that was my name.* "I'm Nellie. What are you doing on my swing?"

"I'm looking for my kokum."

The girl looked at the field. "She's lost?"

Julie nodded.

"Where did you last see her?"

"In her house."

"Oh." Nellie was relieved. "So you're lost."

Julie nodded.

"How old are you?"

"Eight."

"Me too. Do you go to school?"

"I have to be registered first. And that takes time."

"Okay. Do you want some peanut butter sandwiches? I have the crunchy kind."

Julie shook her head.

"My mom can drive you home, she's inside with the baby. But we have a car."

Julie swung her legs out and pumped them. The old swing set rattled and shook.

"You're probably going to break that." But Nellie didn't seem concerned. "You don't want to go home?"

Julie shook her head.

"How come you don't have a hat?" Nellie asked. "You have to have a hat to go outside."

Julie shrugged.

"And you don't have boots." Nellie pointed at her pink rubber boots. "Where are your boots?"

Julie looked down at her sneakers. She remembered when her mom bought them. The flowers had been pink then. Now they were covered in mud. She knocked one foot on top of the other and mud fell to the ground.

"Mom says she will buy boots when her family allowance comes in."

"Where's your mom?"

Julie had been asked that before. A social worker crouched down, slightly off balance and leaning so close to Julie that she could see pepper in her teeth. "Where is your mom?" And then a lady cop. And then another person. And Julie giving the same answer over and over. "She's at the store." That was the answer she was told to give. And, "don't answer the door." And she never did answer it, they let themselves in and she told them she had to wait there. But they didn't listen to her.

"She's at the store."

"Okay. Then you should stay here until she gets back. Do you like checkers?" Nellie asked.

Julie had seen kids playing on TV. "I don't know how."

"Oh it's easy. I can teach you." Nellie moved towards the house.

Julie kept her butt on the swing.

"You have to come inside." Nellie's voice was strict, like an adult.

Julie looked at the woods.

"I can make hot chocolate." Her voice was nicer. "My mom taught me how and we can drink it in my room. I have my own room."

Julie looked down at her shoes. Why did they have to be so cold?

"And I have a TV. And a Nintendo and . . . and . . . dolls? Do you like dolls? I don't like them but if you like them . . . "

Julie liked their smiling round faces and their soft hair. She stopped the swing. She looked at the house. It was green and looked exactly like the house she had come from. Except there was a path leading from the swing-set to the backdoor.

"You're coming?" And then seeing Julie get up, "You're coming!" And her eyes went wide like a kid in the toy aisle at the store. Then she was hurrying up the path.

Julie followed, her eyes on the red coat in front of her.

The Bus Stop

February 1993

Nellie had to wait in the bus stop lobby that was about as much a lobby as this one-horse town was a teeming metropolis. The lobby, if you were determined to call it that, was a short hallway between the front door and the town's only bar, Rascal's. There was no place to sit, unless the floor counted. And Nellie wasn't sitting on that. The carpet was pockmarked where people had thrown down their cigarette butts and ground them into the carpet with their muddy feet.

She couldn't go into Rascal's because even though she'd turned nineteen two weeks before. She'd left her ID back in Saskatoon and her chubby cheeks ensured that she always got ID'd. She could show them her student card and explain that sixty-five percent of first year students towards the end of the second term were nineteen years old. But they could say no and laugh at her and she didn't feel like looking like an idiot in front of the bar staff and whoever else was in there. From the cacophony she was hearing every time the bar door opened, it appeared to be a lot of people or a particularly merry group of chimpanzees. She pulled out a book and leaned against the wall.

After another half hour of waiting, Nellie was sorry that she'd only brought textbooks home with her. She'd already read the pre-history of pre-industrial Europe and a chapter on the Russian Revolution on the bus — that was the interesting stuff — and was now left with Keynesian theory and calculus. She picked up her economics text but couldn't concentrate, not because the book was as dry as month old baked bannock, but because she was pissed.

No I'm just disappointed. Or, I hate this place. Only bad stuff happens here.

Before she'd left the city, she'd called home to the rez. Her fourteen-year-old sister Winona answered the phone, her voice half filled with laughter at something, until she heard heard Nellie's voice.

"What do you want?"

"Where's Mom?"

"At bingo with Dad."

"Tell them I'm coming on Saturday."

"They already know."

"They don't know the time."

"The bus comes only twice a day. You don't need to keep calling."

Nellie reminded herself that she was the mature sister, that she was the one with life experience and could handle a conversation with a little twat.

"Yes but those times are six in the afternoon and midnight. And I'm coming at six in the afternoon and I don't want to be waiting six hours."

"So then you could like call us and we would come get you."

"It's a half hour drive — I don't want to wait that long. Just tell them that I'll be there at six. At the bus stop."

"They already know."

"The time. Tell them the time."

"I'm not your maid."

Nellie could see that her sister was looking for a fight. "How's school?"

"Okay."

"You get into that physics class?"

"Why would I take that?"

"Because I told you that if you want to do medicine then you need to have all three sciences."

"Who said I wanted to be a doctor?"

You did, you obnoxious bitch. When I told everyone that I was going to be a lawyer.

"When you're here, we should go out 'cause Mom and Dad won't let me take out the car anymore."

"I'm not staying long. Only the weekend."

"Don't you have like a whole week off?"

"Yeah, but I have a lot to do in the city."

This was the lie she told everyone. That she went to school, had a job and had loads of friends. Nellie didn't have a job and she had talked to only one girl since she'd gotten to Saskatoon. A girl from a northern reserve who was even shyer than Nellie if that was possible.

She had tried to get the "perfect life." She picked a bar that was the most popular with university students. With its white couches and sparkling lights, Nellie had been intimidated the one night she'd made it inside. She went back in the day time; she stood in the open area with her resumé. The paper shook in the stale air. Great pains had been taken to invent three fake serving jobs. Nellie had never worked as a waitress but she had delivered beers to her dad in the big chair.

She knew she was making a mistake as soon as she saw a blonde waitress hanging out at the bar; at least four inches taller and twenty pounds thinner than Nellie.

But was she as smart as Nellie? Not fucking likely. But did intelligence really matter in the end? Even less fucking likely.

The bartender was talking to another guy. They looked identical. The same blond, cropped, gelled hair. They flirted with the blond Valkyrie. Then a buxom brunette wearing a full face of makeup (and it wasn't even 3:00 PM!) sidled up to the bar and said hi and their attention turned to her.

Try not to judge, Nellie chided herself. *Walk over to them, go, go.* Or not. She waited for them to turn in her direction. They didn't. How could they not see her? She wasn't exactly tiny (although she would be if she would go on that hot pepper and watercress diet that she'd seen in *Glamour* — although hot peppers were expensive and she wasn't sure what watercress was but it sounded like it would be slenderizing). She could feel her hair frizzing out as she stood there. That morning she had curled every single strand trying to emulate Sharon Stone in *Basic Instinct* — but every second she stood here, her hair went from sexy murderer to electrocuted hedgehog.

In an effort to awaken their peripheral vision, Nellie waved her resume as if fanning herself. Nobody acknowledged her. *Oh c'mon, I'm not judging, so you assholes shouldn't either.*

Eventually the girls walked away, the two guys kept chatting. Nellie decided then to make her move. She walked in a bouncy way in hopes that would appear to be perky. She knew she didn't look the way they did but maybe they would overlook that on account of her amazing personality.

Yeah, right. As if.

"Hi. I'm looking for a job?" Her voice went up in an unsure way. Like those girls she sneered at in university when a professor called on them and they weren't ready.

The guys looked at her without seeing her. She held out her resumé and waved it, a token of desperation rather than of peace.

One of the bartenders took the resumé in his hand and looked it over. He nodded. She said something about knowing how to use a cash register. She'd researched cash registers the night before. She was ready for any question. He took a breath and said "We're not hiring right now. But if something changes . . . " He left that part blank, making Nellie think that sometimes people can't be bothered to lie.

Nellie smiled brightly, thinking that if they were trying to go through the motions then she could good-naturedly go through the motions as well. She said thanks with a bright, cold smile that would have made Richard Dawson proud.

Afterwards, she went straight to Dairy Queen and drowned her sorrows in a Peanut Buster Parfait.

She glanced at her watch: an hour and fourteen minutes had passed since the bus had dropped her off and she'd lugged her suitcase inside. That wasn't a long time. Not when you were on your way to pick someone up. But long if you were waiting in a foyer with nothing but an economics book for company. Or punishment. It wasn't her strongest subject. She was sitting at an annoying B minus. But that wasn't her fault. The class was taught by this super-old prof who sucked up to the frat boys who sat at the back of the class and stunk up the room with the booze oozing out of their pores.

In that class, Nellie was a nameless face. A faceless name. Usually she liked that but not when it didn't work in her favour.

A group of men about her dad's age walked into her lobby. She recognized at least one of them as the father of a girl from her high school. They glanced in her direction; she pretended that the theory of supply and demand was the most engrossing thing in the world. As their drunken, horned-up gaze passed over her, she was grateful for her oversized and chunky sweater and the swathe of pimples that made a red rainbow across her forehead.

Nellie glanced out the window. It was snowing. Maybe the roads were bad. Maybe her dad would wander in and explain that he hit the ditch and had to wait for someone to pull him out. He could be in danger. He could be dying.

Nellie went to the telephone booth and dialled — collect — because she didn't have any change and there was no place to get change other than the bar. "Nellie," she said sharply when the automated voice asked for her name. Let them know how angry she was and that they should fucking hurry. It made no matter; the line was busy. She hung up the phone with a loud clang.

At least someone was home. But if one of her sisters was on the phone, she could be stuck for a long time. Maybe they forgot the day. Nellie should have made sure that she talked to her mom; her mom would never forget something like Nellie's homecoming.

Two girls walked in. Nellie recognized them immediately and stuck her nose back into her book. Julie Papequash and Theresa Crookedleg. Her age. She hadn't hung out with them in high school, they took different classes, the ones that ended with "remedial" or "B." And Julie was also one of those floaters, the students who started the year, then transferred to another school mid-year (usually in the city), then transferred back late in the year, usually around May or June. She could never figure that out — how the hell could you get an education if you changed schools twice a year? *And they wonder why they can't keep up!*

The last time she and Julie had hung out together was in elementary school; she smiled all the time but didn't say anything. That had suited Nellie well, she did all the talking. They had been friends until the cool Native girls took Julie and left Nellie behind.

Theresa hadn't been Nellie's friend either. Theresa was a square-faced girl who thought that being mean was the same thing as being confident. Nellie had watched (from a safe distance) as Theresa beat up more than one unlucky girl in the school parking lot. Then she transferred out before the school could expel her.

Expel was a funny word — it sounded like they actually catapulted students out of the school into the wild blue sky. Nellie smiled grimly thinking about how handy a catapult would be right at this moment.

"Nellie?" Julie stopped in front of her, a grin so wide that Nellie knew it was real — although she couldn't figure out how she knew fake from real when hardly anyone smiled at her at all.

"Oh, hi. Sorry, I was reading." Nellie held up her book as proof of her lie.

"You're home."

"For the winter break. Well, we call it Reading Week."

"From university, right?"

"Yeah." *Of course!* Nellie wanted to exclaim, *of course I went to university! How could you not know that? And where the hell else would I have been for the past six months?*

Theresa was staring over Nellie's shoulder at the door to the bar. But Julie was one of those people who took her time no matter who was waiting. "What are you doing there — in university?"

"Pre-law." Nellie waited for the exclamation of her amazingness.

Theresa glanced at Nellie and smacked her gum. "Yeah, I was thinking of doing that."

"Really?" *As if.*

"You waiting around?" Julie asked.

"I'm not waiting, I'm doing what I want with my life."

"I mean here."

Nellie blushed. "Yeah. But my dad should be coming soon."

"I think I hear Everett's laugh!" Theresa exclaimed and hit Julie's shoulder.

Julie rolled her eyes. "That's not him."

"It is!" Theresa tugged on her Julie's arm and Julie allowed herself to be pulled along. She glanced back at Nellie, "Aren't you coming?"

"I'm not old enough."

Theresa snorted, "So what? We haven't been for the last two years."

Julie laughed as well and Nellie made that awkward sound when you wished that laughter could come out of your throat.

They walked ahead and Nellie grabbed her duffel bag, her book bag, her purse and her suitcase in one smooth movement. It was desperation that made her graceful.

As she stepped through the doorway, her eyes darted around the room. It was different than what she thought it would be — mostly smaller. The bar had a low ceiling that made it seem cave-like. Everything was brown or shades of brown. There was a stage, big enough for only the smallest of bands and a dance-floor that could fit fifteen people tops. There was a single bar and a single bartender who looked crowded in by all the liquor bottles. The place smelled like old beer and wet cigarettes — Nellie could feel her stomach flip-flopping with excitement.

Julie walked in front and Theresa and Nellie followed behind her. She meandered from table to table leaning in and saying hi, slapping hands and laughing when someone made a joke.

One of the old guys tried to pull Julie down in his lap. She slapped his hand and kept walking. The men all hooted. "Old pervs!" Julie threw over her shoulder in a laughing voice.

"Quit encouraging them," Theresa hissed at her.

"Free drinks," Julie mouthed back.

Gross but smart, Nellie muttered under her breath.

The waitress came; she'd been a waitress at this bar as long as Nellie could remember. Nellie used to stand at the front door of the bar and look for her dad among the tables. She remembered seeing the same wraith-thin waitress each time. She plopped three beers down on the table, not bothering to ask them for ID.

Nellie studied Julie as she laughed, lit a smoke and took a swig of her beer. In high school, the boys fought over her. Literally. In grade ten, Clarence Simon and Grady Charles slugged it out in the parking lot because Julie didn't know which one she liked better. The incident had left Nellie feeling envious, and contemptuous of teenage boys: *clearly she doesn't like either of you, idiots.*

Nellie never thought Julie was that pretty. *If I lost ten pounds I could look as good as her. And if I could get a decent perm and get contacts that didn't hurt my eyes, and clear up my skin — then I'd be a slightly thinner, poodle-haired, squinty eyed, starving maniac.*

It was hard to find a flaw on Julie's face. Even a zit only called attention to how pretty she was.

"Are you dating Everett?" Nellie blurted out.

Julie nodded at Theresa who was now glaring at Nellie. "She's the lucky lady."

"Why do you want to know about Everett?" The lucky lady snarled.

"We all went to school together, remember?"

"Uh huh and you like other women's men?"

"I was wondering what happened to him." Nellie's eyes flicked over Theresa's crooked teeth. "And now I know."

Julie looked away but Nellie could see her smile.

"I'll tell him you were asking about him. I'm sure he'll find that funny."

"Good, I like to make people laugh." Nellie could feel how close she was to getting punched in the face. She took a sip of beer in defiance of her desire to run screaming out of the building, into the snowstorm, where she would hide until she learned not to piss off people meaner and stronger than her.

Luck was in Nellie's favour. Someone waved at Theresa and she got up to talk to them. Theresa didn't tell them that or anything, she just got up with a bang and left. Nellie dodged a vicious swing of her purse as she went by.

"She's interesting," Nellie commented.

"I don't talk about people behind their back." Julie's voice was calm.

Nellie felt her face go red. She wanted to defend herself but didn't know what to say. Because if Julie had been into it, she would have ripped Theresa into a thousand pieces. Now she had no place to put her anxiety.

Julie took pity on her. "What's your favourite part of university?"

Nobody had ever asked Nellie that before. She thought about it. "I guess all the choices. You can literally learn about anything. Like I could've taken the history of the Americas or the history of China or Africa and I was kinda freakin' myself out because I couldn't figure out which one I wanted. Then I waited too long and by the time I went to register only history of Europe was open. But I really like it because the class isn't about the royalty and the lords and all that — it's about how the regular people lived — well, they called them peasants back then — " Nellie stopped talking like she'd been unplugged. She should know better than to talk long about stuff like picking her classes.

People's eyes would glaze over and they got mad that she was dominating the conversation. But Julie didn't seem mad, she seemed to be listening.

"What are you doing?" Nellie asked because she honestly wanted to know. "Weren't you interested in hair or something?"

Julie nodded, "Yeah, I went to work in a salon in town here and turns out I'm allergic to all the chemicals. Makes my skin swell."

"Plan B?"

"Only had the one plan." Julie moved her body to the beat of "Copperhead Road", a song that Nellie remembered coming from the cars in the parking lot at their school all the time. There was something about being from a fucked up place that hit a note with these people. She looked over at the dented jukebox. Someone had taken the boots to it — but it was still cranking out the tunes. Good thing. *If that thing ever broke, people would have to listen to each other.*

Nellie didn't have anything to say so she sucked back her beer.

She'd never liked the taste of beer but it tasted different in a bar sitting across from someone her age. After she finished that beer, some more were ordered (they didn't pay for those ones either). By her third, there were lots of people sitting around their table. Lots of guys. Nellie joked with them and they laughed and she felt like, *wow there is nothing wrong with me.*

When her mom finally showed up around midnight, Nellie was sorry to leave. She stood up and went around the table to hug Julie.

"You should come visit me in the city", she urged Julie. "Anytime you want."

The House

April 1993

EVERETT'S MOM HAD MENTAL problems. That's what everyone told him. That's why when Everett was six they moved from the city back to the rez. They moved into his uncle's house with his wife and his two boys. Everett shared a twin mattress with his mom in the basement. It smelled weird down there — like wet blankets and spiders. ("Oh go on, spiders have no smell." "But they do, Mom.") Everett got used to it. Started to love it, even, because it was completely black at night and cold so she held him close and called him her "little man."

While the ceiling above creaked with everyone walking around, his mom would tell him stories about his grandfather and his great grandfather. They were warriors and chiefs and medicine men. She told him about how his great-grandfather had his first Raindance when he was fifty years old because that was when the spirits told him to do it. She told him how everyone in the village teased him for acting like he was younger than he was. Why is an old man having his Raindance now? They asked. "He had to follow the spirits," his mother whispered in Everett's ear. "Everything happens when it's supposed to."

When he was ten years old, he came home from school and his mom was sitting in the kitchen with a knapsack beside her feet. It was a kid's backpack and had Big Bird on the front of it. She said she would come back for him "once she got on her feet." And he tried to think what that meant.

He followed her to the door but he didn't cling because he was her little man.

"When you coming home?"

"By Christmas, I promise."

And then she kissed him on the lips and he could feel her tears on his face and he waited for her that Christmas but she never came back and his uncle made sure that he got the same number of presents as his cousins that year.

After that, Everett slept on the same mattress but his uncle helped him carry it from the basement into the boys' room, because his uncle told him he would turn out weird if he slept in the basement by himself. His aunt used to tuck his mattress under her boys' bunk bed when they went to school. And then when everyone was ready to go to bed, Everett would pull it out again. He learned how to go to sleep after everyone else and when his head hit the pillow he was out like a light because he knew had to be the first up in the morning or else the boys would step on him, sometimes by accident, sometimes because they thought it was funny. He learned to laugh along to everything because when you're the extra kid you can't make trouble.

When he got older and he found out how easy it was to get girls, he had more places to stay. He would sleep at a girlfriend's house until her parents got sick of him hanging around and then he'd head back to his uncle's. "Thought we lost you that time for sure," his aunt would say.

His cousins moved out on the same day, Eric, the older one, went to BC for school and Jason joined the Army. Everett would have had the bedroom to himself but it didn't feel right so he moved out the next day too.

He piled his stuff in the back of his pickup truck and drove to Saskatoon. He heard that was where everyone went plus it only cost one tank of gas to get there. Once he got to the city, he realized he needed a place to stay so he called a guy from the rez that he used to play hockey with. The guy told him that his old lady didn't like people staying over and gave Everett the address of the Salvation Army: "They got food and you can sleep there for free."

Everett parked in front and rang the doorbell. A sleepy-eyed brunette with a bossy voice opened the door and told him he could stay but to not come after curfew again.

"Got it," Everett said with a big grin. She smiled back shyly as she handed him a pillow and a blanket. She led him to a dorm room with six sets of bunk beds. Bodies were everywhere and in the light from the hallway, Everett saw dozens of suspicious eyes on him. He threw himself onto an upper bunk and slept immediately.

Everett woke up the next morning and saw that most of the stuff he brought with him had been stolen from the back of his pickup. *Like a fucking free-for-all.* His mattress was still there though, looking like grey oatmeal half-filling up the truck's box.

He went back inside and had breakfast. A skinny guy about his age told him that there was a construction site looking for young guys like him.

"I don't know anything about construction," Everett said in between mouthfuls of scrambled eggs and bacon and toast and hash browns.

"You just need to have hands."

Everett asked him for the address and offered the skinny dude a ride to the site.

"Nah, I'm not working right now," the young guy said, "I'm taking a break." Everett noticed then how the guy's wrist bones protruded and how his teeth had turned brown and spindly.

Everett drove to the site after breakfast. The foreman looked him over with interest. "Can you cut your hair?"

Everett's hair was half way down his back. "Why?"

"Kinda dangerous on a site."

"Guess so."

Everett started that day. He carried lumber from place to place for the first part of the morning. Then they paired him with an older carpenter with wind and sun etched into his face. Mike's handshake was fierce.

"So are you the kind of Indian that works hard or the kind that wastes my fucking time?"

"Works-hard-kind."

"I can make you a great carpenter, is that what you want?"

Everett grinned.

Everett had never liked working with his hands. He'd taken shop but almost failed. That may have also been because the shop class had a photography darkroom attached where Everett spent most of his time fooling around with girls. It was so dark in there, sometimes he forgot who he was with. Part of the game was trying to remember her name before the lights came up.

"What reserve you from?"

"Stone Man."

Mike laughed, "That's a helluva name for a reserve. You move off because you got tired of being stoned all the time?"

Everett shrugged.

"Where you living?"

"Salvation Army."

"What a shithole."

"Food's good."

"I got a house, lots of room. Long as you work here, you can live with me."

Everett moved his mattress in to an empty bedroom on the second floor of Mike's house and threw it on the middle of the floor. He piled his clothes in the corner. He sat on the mattress and stared at the window. He couldn't see much of the city, only the sky. He could hear Mike downstairs playing on his guitar.

The sound was low and easy and Everett felt like he had a soundtrack to his life. Everett figured he would eventually get around to asking Mike to teach him how to play. But two days later, Mike went over to his ex-girlfriend's house and shot her.

Everett was up early that morning when the police came. They knocked on the door while Everett was making toast. Mike wasn't up yet which should have told Everett that something was wrong.

The knocking got loud and even though Everett felt weird answering someone else's door, he walked over and let the police in.

When they asked for Michael Bennett, Everett stared at them wordlessly because he didn't even know Mike's full name. Plus there were more cops than he'd ever seen in his life — so he stood there with his mouth hanging open. One of them pushed him up against a wall and Everett felt metal against his skin (he wasn't wearing a shirt). They demanded his name.

"Everett," he croaked and then laughed because he couldn't believe how scared he was.

Mike came out of his bedroom about then. He was wearing a nice shirt, not a work-shirt. He told the police to leave Everett alone.

As Mike was led out the door in cuffs, he said to Everett: "Watch my house."

Everett nodded. Then he went back to bed.

Things That Can Be Taken

October 1993

Julie SHOWED UP IN the middle of the night — "That was when the bus got in, Nellie" — and woke up Nellie and her roommate, Shaylene, whom Nellie wasn't even speaking to because Shaylene refused to do her dishes and she never turned off her stupid TV even when she went to bed.

Shaylene opened her bedroom door as Nellie walked past and gave Nellie a meaningful glare before she slammed it shut again.

Nellie was huffy when she opened the front door. "I thought you were coming tomorrow."

"I didn't read the schedule right." Julie shifted her duffel bag from just outside the door, to just inside.

Nellie figured she should do something nice like offer Julie a pop or a beer or something to eat but she had a psychology mid-term in the morning and that was her best class — she was literally at the top of it, like out of 600 other students, and she wasn't giving that up because someone couldn't figure out a stupid bus schedule.

"Okay, well, the couch pulls out and here's a blanket. You can use this one as a pillow or one of those couch pillows or your jacket or something. We have pillows somewhere but I don't know where my roommate put them."

"Where's your roommate?"

"Hear the TV? That's her."

Julie's eyes strayed to the empty TV stand in the living room. "She keeps the TV in her bedroom?"

"It's hers."

Julie nodded but her eyes were confused.

"Do you know where you're going tomorrow?"

"The SIAST campus."

"Okay, well, good night."

Nellie slipped back underneath her comforter. There was no sound from the living room. *At least, no sound that couldn't be heard above the sound of her roommate's fucking TV.*

Nellie waited for sleep to pull her under. And waited. She thought about how her mom said she was supposed to welcome guests into a house with a meal and even leave the door open for them so they could let themselves in. Nellie should have asked Julie if she wanted to sleep with her. *Then we could have stayed up late giggling and talking about boys and her trip and all that. But no, I stomp to the door and stomp back to bed. This is the way I ruin every moment and that's why I have no friends. But shouldn't I have friends who are like me anyways? But would I even like someone who was like me?* Nellie thought about taking a sleeping pill but they always made her groggy in the morning and when she took them she felt like she was going to have a stroke — putting stuff into your brain to slow it down couldn't be good for you.

When Nellie got up the next morning, Julie was asleep on the couch. She hadn't bothered to pull it out. Her feet, small for a tall person, stuck out over the arm of the couch. Her head perched on the other. Nellie was ninja-quiet heading out the door but when she turned the handle, she heard a soft "have a good day" and Nellie wanted to turn around and do something nice. But what? Kiss Julie on the forehead like she was a child and Nellie was her mom? Um, no, then she'd look crazy. Nellie hurried up the steps; she liked being early to class because then she got the best seat.

❦❦❦

Nellie meant to go right home after her exam but then she remembered that she had to meet with her economics prof Mr. Wolski.

He had a grad student teaching his tutorial, a tall, bearded pompous ass. Nellie and he had knocked heads since day one when she corrected his pronunciation of Keynsian. Then she saw him holding hands outside the grad student lounge with Alexandra, a Russian immigrant first-year with white-blond hair, small eyes and big tits.

Nellie told the prof that she wanted to make sure that everyone was getting the same help. The professor had his arms folded when she sat down and pretty much kept them that way until Nellie started citing university policy about student/teacher relations.

"It's too late to get another grad student," he said finally.

Nellie stared at him and kept her mouth shut. She'd learned that if you stayed quiet it made people nervous.

"I mean I know what he's done is definitely bad and likely a conflict of interest but he's doing a good job, no one else has complained."

Nellie brought her index finger to her mouth and chewed. She didn't actually chew her fingernails, but she thought it made her look vulnerable. Mr. Wolski was about fifty, maybe older, because he had those brown spots on his hands that said old-old. His eyes were red in the white parts. But there was a tennis racquet lying in a corner of his office so she knew he worked out. Nellie wondered which student he was sleeping with.

She took her finger out of her mouth. "The thing is Mr. Wolski, I don't want to get anyone in trouble but I also don't want to get in trouble myself for not reporting what I know."

The professor sighed. His chair squeaked mightily as he straightened himself out. The hair on the back of Nellie's neck stood up — it meant either you were about to get hit or you were about to get your way. He leaned forward and Nellie forced herself to remain motionless.

"I think we can settle this between us."

❧❧❧

Nellie walked down the hallway at a brisk pace. Partly because of her excitement, partly because she felt like if she walked too slow the prof would come out of his office and throw something at the back of her head. But even a possible concussion couldn't change the facts — she was in second year and she was teaching an economics tutorial. She wanted to stop people and yell it into their faces.

Instead she steadfastly avoided eye contact with anyone in the hallway and went directly to the library to check on her holds. She was distracted by a book in the "New Books" display about serial killers. She enjoyed reading about them, even thought she might make a good FBI profiler (if it paid well enough). But she tried not to read too many serial killer books because after a while she started seeing everyone as a possible murderer — like her roommate, for instance, who *was* secretive and manipulative. Then again, Shaylene was also a real slob and serial killers tended to be anal and neat. They would probably make decent roommates.

Nellie signed out her library books and headed to her favourite study carrel. It was on the seventh floor, which was second to last. The last floor was where fuckheads went to fuck each other. She preferred the cool, quiet seventh floor where people studied. She cracked a book and turned off the world. The next time she checked her watch, it was after eight. She piled her books in her backpack along with a bag of Ruffles she'd snuck into the library. It kept her from having to go down to the cafeteria and eating down there with all those sneering assholes staring openly at her second hand clothes and her bulging backpack.

She caught the bus — it was empty except for some trades dudes who smelled like gasoline and had black smeared hands. A guy with two missing front teeth and grey hair smiled at her. She gave him a crooked smile. *Maybe you can save me. Maybe we can move into the rooming house where you live with six other old guys like you with tight bodies and craggy faces and slowly drink ourselves to death.*

Her eyes locked with his and he looked away.

Nellie turned towards the window and smiled at the tired girl looking back at her. That was the most sexual attention she'd had in months. She made another mental note to kill the hairdresser who had given her the shitty perm.

Nellie heard a strange sound coming from her apartment; it was laughter. Nellie stopped outside and took a deep breath before opening the door.

She opened the door. Julie sat on the couch and Shaylene sat in front of her on the floor. It looked like Julie was grooming her roommate like a chimpanzee and then Nellie saw that she was actually braiding her hair. Those tiny braids that took forever.

"Hi," Nellie tried to speak over the volume of the TV.

Julie flashed her pretty teeth. "Wow, you bring home the whole library?"

Nellie disentangled her backpack from her arms, "Just half." It dropped to the floor with a thud.

She stared at the TV. It was in the living room on the stand that had stood empty for the last three months. Nellie's eyes eagerly ate up the bright colours of a *Simpsons* episode.

Nellie dragged her eyes away. "How was your day?"

Julie made a face. "They won't let me register. The school says the band never sent the money for tuition. So no student-Julie."

"That's awful! Did you call them?" Nellie would have complained until someone cried and then she would have mowed through those tears until she got her way.

Julie shrugged. "No biggie. It's my first time being here. I wouldn't mind seeing more of the city before I get serious."

"But you don't have any money." *And you can't stay here for free.*

"She has a job." Shaylene's eyes shone and her lip was curled like she knew the punchline to a joke Nellie hadn't heard.

"It's a waitressing job."

"At Lorette's." Shaylene's smile was as bright as *The Simpsons'* opening credits.

"That's a good place." Nellie picked up her book bag and walked it to her room.From behind her she heard Julie call out, "You want something to eat? I made rice."

"No," Nellie yelled through her closing bedroom door.

She sat on her bed and saw herself in her full-length mirror. Red faced, brown curly hair cut into a shape of some sort, glasses sliding down that oil slick she called skin. When was the butterfly supposed to emerge? She snorted.

She stood up, walked up close to the mirror, pulled up her shirt. Tummy, lots of it. She grabbed a fat roll and pinched it. "Gross, so fucking gross."

Nellie had thought about getting a knife and cutting into her belly, and pulling the fat out and dumping it out on the floor.

Emergency could sew her back up; that was their job, right? She might be horribly scarred but she would be thin.

But what about her face? That would still be fat and plain and pimpled and all those things that made people's eyes pass over her.

The door opened. Nellie dropped her shirt. She covered the movement by pretending to massage her waist. Julie slipped inside the room. "What?" Nellie's voice suggested that she was intruding.

"It's just me." Julie dropped herself on Nellie's bed and leaned against the wall. "You wanna go out? Sort of celebrate my escape from the rez?"

"I have a lot of homework."

"You know Everett lives in town, right?"

"Yeah, I see him all the time. He helped us move our couch." *Well, he lent us his truck.*

"I saw him today — "

"Where?"

"Downtown, near the bus stop, and he said he was having a party tonight. You wanna go?"

Nellie's fatigue was washed away like sand beneath an ocean wave "Sure, whatever."

Nellie could feel her heart beating faster so she reached beneath her bed and pulled out four beers on a ring. Julie laughed.

"You have beer under your bed?"

"Sometimes I have one before I go to sleep."

"Smart."

They opened them at the same time. There was barely a pop.

"Shaylene says she's gonna stay in. She doesn't drink, huh?"

"Nope."

"So what's happening with Everett?" Julie smiled up at Nellie.

"Nothing. I mean we kissed a few times but everyone kisses Everett. He's community property." *But not forever . . .*

"Same ole Everett."

"He doesn't work, y'know. He does odd jobs and stuff. 'Cause he doesn't have to pay rent — "

"'Cause he lives in the house of a guy who went to jail."

They laughed.

"Only Everett."

"Yeah, no kidding. Guy has a horseshoe up his ass and then some."

Nellie dressed carefully. Something fitted but not tight — something that made her look skinny — skinny-ish. And definitely a blue scarf because colour near her face made her look less tired. And if they were walking home tomorrow morning, it wouldn't look so obvious. They could be anyone, headed to the farmer's market, going to the library to return some library books, off to brunch — or they could be two hungover Native chicks heading home — the sky was the limit.

Julie wore a pair of sneakers, jeans and a KISS T-shirt. Nellie wanted to change — her clothes, her hair, her genetic destiny. Instead, she finished her beer with a final gulp and tossed it.

"You look amazing!" Shaylene gushed at Julie. "How do you stay so skinny?"

"I'm too fucking skinny. I wish I could gain weight."

"You're so lucky."

Julie smiled and nodded as her eyes studied some crud on the counter. Nellie understood that look. It's what she did when people complimented her on her grades. Because there was nothing you could really say. What other people wanted came naturally to Julie and they weren't complimenting her so much as expressing their desire to have it. (Of course Nellie's grades were something she had to work for but she tried not to let anyone know about that part. Why ruin the illusion and destroy the one thing she had over other people?)

"We should go."

"Are you sure you don't want to come?" Julie asked Shaylene.

"I don't like parties."

"For real?" Julie cocked her head to the side.

Shaylene put her fist to her mouth and nodded.

Nellie poked Julie in the back. "We should go, bus is coming."

Nellie walked fast but Julie had no problem keeping up.

"What's with Shaylene? Is she like religious or something?"

"She used to go to parties at Everett's house but then she got raped."

"Oh. Did they catch the guy?"

"She never charged him."

"Who is he?"

"A southern rez guy. If he's there, I'll point him out."

"That's fucked up."

"I know."

"Did you tell Everett?"

"Shaylene doesn't want anyone to know."

"We'll watch each other's backs, okay?"

Nellie had that feeling again, like she wanted to grab Julie's hand and squeeze it. Instead she thought about how tall and thin Julie's shadow looked next to hers and how she should try that lemon and pepper diet she saw in the back of *Cosmo* magazine and this time she would stay on it no matter how hungry she got. No pain, no gain.

There were three guys sitting on the front steps when they walked up. Everett, Gary and some other guy Nellie had never seen before. He was ugly. *No, be nice Nellie; he's just "not cute."* Everett stood up as soon as he saw them and came bounding up to them. "It's the girls!"

The girls. Not girls. The girls. Like as if no other girls in the world mattered.

"You got a liquor store nearby?" Julie asked.

Everett shook his head. "Don't worry about it. These guys just got paid." Everett introduced them: Gary had been staying with Everett for a couple of weeks, he worked at the post office. The less than handsome guy's name was Chris and he was an ironworker.

"Like those Mohawk guys that work on the skyscrapers?" Julie asked.

"Yeah, 'cept there's no skyscrapers here," Chris drawled. He leaned backwards to take in all of Julie, his legs splayed in front of him.

Nellie noticed this because she'd read a magazine article on attraction and when men were attracted to a woman they unconsciously made themselves bigger and women did the opposite. Nellie noticed that Julie's posture remained unchanged. *Too bad for you, Chris.*

They sat on the steps and the boys made them laugh with their work stories. Everett changed jobs every few months so he had the most. He'd just finished a stint at the water treatment plant. "Guys piss in the drinking water all the time," he said. "Half the water you're drinking is some asshole's pee."

"That's why I stick to beer," Julie joked.

"I heard that all of our drinking water is recycled through at least four bladders," Chris said. Everyone looked grossed out.

"Wouldn't it be an infinite number of bladders?" Nellie asked. "Because, you know, it's the same water that's always been around."

There was a long pause. Long enough for Nellie to feel her neck turning pink.

"Nerd." Everett leaned forward and poked her in the tummy.

Nellie wondered how it would be when they were married. Like would he start reading more? Maybe they could take a class together. She didn't want to have stupid kids. But she would love them no matter what.

A cop car drove by slowly so they took the party inside. They decided on a game of poker. Nellie talked them out of strip poker. Not because she was shy or prudish but she could tell that she was not the main attraction.

Think positive Nellie, remember what Oprah says, the right man will find you, you just have to live your own life until that happens. And get drunk a lot in the meantime, because what else are you going to do? Everett went to get the cards, the other guys stayed by the cupboards where they discussed motors and other boring things.

Nellie opened another beer. She watched the foam pour out the beer and slide down the side.

"Watcha thinking?" Julie perched on the counter next to Nellie, her long legs double crossed.

"I got a teaching job at the university today."

"That's great!"

"I blackmailed my teacher."

"What does that mean?"

"It means I made him do what I wanted by using information against him."

"I thought that was a ransom."

"No that's when you take someone or something from someone and then you make them pay you to give it back."

"God I'm such an idiot." Julie laughed. Nellie could feel the guys' attention turning towards the sound. It was a pretty laugh.

"It's sort of the same thing."

"I wish I had half your brains."

I wish I had all my brains and all of your beauty. And you had nothing.

Nellie ran her index finger across the sharp part of the can's mouth. "Yeah, but now my professor hates me."

"When you take what people want, of course they're gonna hate you. But they'll respect you. And that's good, right?"

Nellie nodded. "That's what *Death of a Salesman* said."

Julie smiled, nodded and shrugged all at the same time.

There were times when Nellie would drink and it would feel like she never got drunk. Like everyone was laughing and joking and she was locked on the outside pounding to get into the warmth of the good time. This was one of those nights. She could still feel the pain when the boys gathered back into the room and Everett made sure to sit next to Julie and Chris made sure to pull his chair in between Nellie and Julie. Then when the drinking games started, Nellie threw herself into them with an enthusiasm bordering on hysteria. She crowed when people lost, stood and chanted, "drink drink drink!"

She pounded on the table with her fist, spilling drinks every-where — she didn't care, she was a warrior. When Everett told her to "relax," she told him "to quit being a little bitch."

Her fervour blew the party's fire out. She tried to bring the embers back by joking around but her jokes were harsh ones, about bad teeth and greasy hair, and nobody laughed.

She got the couch. It looked directly at Everett's bedroom door. Not at the TV. And she sat there stubbornly staring at that door. Any second now, any second now. He was going to walk outside and sit next to her and tell her that he was putting Julie to bed, that he was doing it because he was the nicest of guys. Nellie felt a pain that settled over her entire body, into her bones so deep that it linked with other hurts stored there where they melded and made her into stone. *I am paralyzed.* She tried to scream but couldn't. Instead she sat and stared.

She woke to someone's hand on her boob. Expert-like, it teased her nipple. She felt a tongue in her mouth. *He came for me. But wait, after he was with her? That's not right. But still, can't I have this? Maybe he'll change his mind when he sees how . . .*

Nellie realized it was not Everett's tongue in her mouth. Not that tongues are that easy to identify. But she knew.

Without opening her eyes, she went for the throat. One quick punch and the guy fell backwards. As she hopped over him, she saw Chris rolling beside the couch hissing the word, "bitch" at her as she rushed for the bathroom. She locked the door. Her shirt was gaping open. She quickly buttoned it with shaking fingers. She noticed a button missing where he'd impatiently groped her. She checked her jeans. Still clasped shut. She gulped back some bile.

There was a knock at the bathroom door. A whispered, "Nellie?"

"Go fuck yourself," she growled out. She knew what voice to make, what tone, what volume. It wasn't her first time on the merry go round with some disgusting fuck.

Focus on something else.

I want to go home. The thought was red and capitalized. Now.

Nellie looked at the bathroom window. She opened it and looked down. The sidewalk was one quick jump away. She saw the concrete wind around to the front of the house. There would be no bus but she could walk it. She would stay to the shadows, duck into alleys if she saw people or the police — she'd heard the stories about them. She hooked her purse over her shoulder and jumped. Easy peasy. She would be tired but she would be safe in her bed before the night was over.

৵৵৵

Julie came home around eight that night. *Not her home, I should kick her skinny ass out.*

Nellie had heard the phone ring earlier, saw the number come up as "M. Bennett" — Everett's number (he never bothered to change the number from that guy who murdered his ex-girlfriend) — and ignored it. She had nothing to say.

Nellie had thought about stopping in Shaylene's room and sitting on the edge of the bed and telling her. But what? "I escaped."

Instead Nellie climbed into the shower and washed everything away. Threw up in the toilet and showered again. She wrapped herself in her big yellow comforter and sat on her bed with her knees to her chest. *I want my mom.* But what would she say? Because talking meant telling.

So she read — a chapter of biology, then micro economics, then the history of the western world (two chapters). Then she fell asleep. Then she had a peanut butter sandwich. She let herself watch one episode of *The Simpsons* (they played three in a row on Sunday afternoons.) She stopped watching because it was where the neighbour's wife dies. *I just want to laugh today, idiot writers.* She tossed the remote control onto the coffee table where it made a slight dent (their coffee table was two twenty four beer boxes taped together).

She did more readings. She started drafting a fifteen-page paper that was due in three weeks. She made a research schedule for herself. She ate seven cookies. Then fell asleep, face down, her feet hanging off the bed.

About half an hour into Nellie's nap, Julie slipped into her bedroom. She hadn't made a sound as she walked in and turned on the light, she was a ninja too that one. Nellie sat up and wiped at the drool at the corner of her mouth. They stared at each other, unsure of what the other was thinking.

"My head hurts." Julie did look pale.

"Mine too."

"So you studying?"

"Yeah."

"I have to go to work tonight."

"Right."

Julie stroked one of Nellie's scarves hanging from the closet door. "So you guys are okay with me staying here?"

No. I hate you.

"It's fine."

"'Cause he asked me to move in with him . . . but I like it here. With girls. I mean, it's *Everett*, I shouldn't have messed with him. God, why do guys have to be so clingy?"

"Yeah." Nellie stared down at her pen.

"You ever been to this Lorette's? Shaylene says it's pretty busy."

"Yup, it's the place to go. You'll make lots in tips."

"Why don't you get a job there? Then we could work together."

Nellie was too tired to lie. "I applied. But they didn't call me. You know how it is. With faces and stuff."

Julie ran her nail over a drip of dried paint on the closet door, sticking the tip of it into the bubble and peeling it off. "I'll steal from the till for you then."

Nellie smiled for the first time that day.

Stranger Danger

March 1994

He was taking Julie to a restaurant.

"What if it's someplace fancy, like The Keg? Like holee what am I gonna do then?" Then, thinking it made her sound like her head was big, she added: "I mean, as if, right? Like he's gonna take an Indian to some fancy restaurant?"

"But what if he does? And what if it's somewhere even fancier like that steakhouse in the Delta Bess or someplace so expensive that we've never even heard of it!" Nellie was a fan of raising every single terrifying possibility.

"I won't go in then."

"Of course you'll go in! What are you gonna do, sit in the car like a nutcase?"

"I would." And Nellie knew she would; she'd seen Julie's shyness stiffen her spine enough times.

Julie tried on all of her clothes. Then raided Nellie's closet.

Then Shaylene's. They didn't mind. There was a mountain of homework to be done but this eclipsed all of that.

"I hate it when guys ask you out on dates, like why can't you just hang out?" Shaylene said. "I would literally be crawling under the table."

Nellie turned her head away from them so that she could roll her eyes properly and thoroughly. As if anyone would ever ask out Shaylene. She'd been cute once but now she never left the apartment, like ever, and she ordered pizza every single day. Nellie would tell her, "You're turning into a pizza," which wasn't nice but it was true. Shaylene smelled like pizza, was round like one and even her face was dotted with red marks like pieces of salami. Nellie had to squint to see the smart-assed biology major from Witcheken Lake she'd met in her first week of university.

Julie stuck her tongue at the face in the mirror. "Should I curl my hair?"

"No." Nellie and Shaylene said at the same time. Easy answer. Her hair was a black cascade of shiny perfection. But then Nellie had a thought.

"White girls curl their hair."

"Yeah, so?"

"You already look straight out Native, maybe you can look a little less. Like wearing jeans instead of a buckskin skirt."

"Who the fuck owns a buckskin skirt?"

"You know what I mean."

"You're racist," Shaylene piped up.

"I'm not racist. I'm saying he's a white guy and you're Native. You already look like salt and pepper, why make it obvious?"

"Curling my hair isn't gonna make me fucking Barbie."

"But it'll make you less Poca-fucking-hontas."

"No way, it takes forever and the curl falls out anyway."
Julie sighed. "Fuck. What am I gonna wear?"

"Those jeans, this shirt." Nellie had it all worked out; she
tossed the outfit on the bed. Julie studied them.

"That is a nerd outfit."

"You're nineteen. Time to dress more grown up," Shaylene
said firmly. Nellie was surprised. Shaylene never backed her
up on anything.

Two against one. Julie pulled on the button up shirt. It was
Nellie's and was a bit baggy on Julie, except in the boob area
where her breasts strained to break free from their corral.

Having Julie around was like peering into the world of
movie stars. Nellie hadn't realized that men really do stop
women on the street and ask them to dinner until she started
hanging out with Julie. Though when it happened, nine times
out of ten, Julie would look past the guy at a point in the
distance and snap her gum until he finally felt stupid enough
to walk away.

But not this guy, he had waited until Julie made eye
contact. He told her his name was Neil. Julie mumbled her
name back while staring at the bus stop schedule. He asked
her out to dinner and even though she looked like she'd rather
set herself on fire, she said "yeah" woodenly. When he kept
standing there, Nellie took pity on him and gave him their
number and address.

When they were on the bus, Julie asked her why she stuck
her big nose in and Nellie replied that she thought it would
make an interesting experiment.

"You look great. Like Julie but a grown up version. It's like
you have a job and a car or something."

"Ha, whatever, Shrimp. I look ugly."

Nellie had never heard that word out of Julie's mouth. "You should wear a purse."

"Nope, I forget them all over the place."

Nellie insisted. "Women wear purses."

Julie didn't, she tucked her ID in her back pocket. Once Nellie was standing next to her in a bar bathroom mirror and Julie pulled a tube of lip gloss out of her bra. (Nellie thought it was the coolest thing she ever saw.) Nellie went everywhere weighed down with a heavy purse filled with makeup, hairspray, snacks and a book.

Nellie transferred Julie's worldly goods — gum, twenty bucks and her pink lip gloss — into her spare purse and hung it over Julie's shoulder. "You look like a preppy Asian girl."

"Except she's not rich and not in the College of Engineering." Shaylene was really enjoying this.

Julie flopped onto Nellie's bed. "I don't wanna go. I'm gonna call him and tell him I have the shits."

"You have to go. It's a real date!" The closest Nellie had ever come to that was when Everett asked her to meet him at McDonald's. She still had to pay for her Big Mac though. And his.

"You guys should come."

"I'm sure it's every white guy's dream to date three Native girls at the same time, but no." Not that Nellie knew anything about white guys. She barely talked to anyone in her classes other than, "what mark did you get?" or "how long did you study?" or if she was feeling frisky, "sure is cold outside."

"My palms are sweating."

"That's 'cause you like him."

Julie made a face at Nellie. "No it's 'cause this is stupid and I don't know why you're making me do it."

A car horn beeped.

"Oh fuck that's him."

"Why isn't he coming in?"

"I told him not to."

Nellie was disappointed, she wanted to see him again. She liked how he talked in complete sentences. She needed more practise around people like that.

Julie reluctantly got to her feet and paused in front of the mirror leaning against the wall. Nellie had it angled to make her look as skinny as possible so Julie looked like a runway model in it.

"You look beautiful," Shaylene said breathlessly.

"I don't wanna go."

Nellie gave her a shove. "For fuck sakes, get out of here!"

"Fuck you." Julie shoved her back. But she went. The girls followed her to the front door and watched as she trudged down the steps. They saw as she spit her gum out near the front steps and got into the car. They watched even as his car pulled away.

Nellie felt the same wild curiosity that had driven her to lick a metal pole, many winters ago.

ঙ৲ঙ৲ঙ৲

Nellie was struggling with an English paper. Her professor had said at the beginning of class: "There are no right answers only answers that you are able to support." Nellie hated open-ended shit. She just wanted to know which argument would give her an A.

She called Everett. There was no answer. He had no answering machine but he had call display which showed how many times she called. Right now, if he bothered to glance at it, he would see: twelve.

She had been angry six calls ago. Now she was disappointed. And horny.

She opened up her political science binder, it was filled with photocopied readings. She had to read about Aristotle even though she'd already read about him in philosophy. It must be nice to straddle two subjects with the same boring writing. She went to the kitchen to refill her tea. She was drinking green tea these days, it was supposed to fire up her metabolism by getting rid of all the free radicals lurking in her body. She didn't know what those were but Oprah said they were bad. Nellie hadn't lost a pound but then again it was hard to eat healthy when the entire apartment smelled like pizza.

Nellie padded into the kitchen and saw a pizza container on the counter. She squelched a scream of frustration.She opened the pizza box; it was sausage and pepperoni. The top of the box was rimmed in dark where the fat had soaked into the cardboard.

Nellie spit on the pizza and spread the spit over the top of it with her finger. She was closing the box carefully when the front door opened.

She looked around the corner as Julie stalked past her. Nellie hurried behind her.

Julie sat on Nellie's bed, her back against the wall, her legs stretched in front of her. Julie's bedroom was the living room so during the day she used Nellie's. It wasn't the best situation but Nellie didn't feel like giving up the extra rent money.

Nellie started small. "Did you have fun?"

"I guess."

"Did you make out with him?"

"No."

"Did you want to?"

Julie made a damn-I-stepped-in-dog-poop-and-I'm-wearing-sandals-face.

"Okay then." Nellie's disappointment was writ clear.

"He wants to see me this weekend. So I told him I work this weekend and then he's all like what about before work and so I said yes to get out of the car." Julie turned her gaze to the ceiling. "He wants to hang out at the park — what the fuck is at the park?"

"There's ducks."

"You and Everett ever go to the park?"

Nellie and Everett never went anywhere together. It was her house or his. Sometimes she saw him at the bar and she would wave to him and he would act like he was going to come over but he never got to where she was sitting.

One time she asked him to meet her at Place Riel at the university. She saw other girls meet their boyfriends there.

She explained to him how to get there, walked him through the streets one by one. He never showed up. He told her that he made it to the University Bridge but then some woman gave him a weird look which made him feel weird so he turned around and went home.

"I don't like ducks," Nellie replied.

"There wasn't a single Indian in that place. Me and a bunch of white people. I felt like everyone was looking at us and I couldn't stop looking at his arms. He had this blonde hair all over them. Like lots of it." Julie made a face that she saved for the smell of rotten garbage.

"That's how white people are." How would Nellie know? She'd never studied one up close. "Was he nice?"

"He asked me if I liked being called Indian or Native."

"Always say Native."

"I know that, Nellie. But I don't have to answer that question if I'm with an Indian guy."

Nellie wanted to argue from the perspective of diversity and being open minded but she was tired and felt nauseated from the smell of pizza. So, they walked down to the Rainbow Cinema where movies were three dollars on Sunday afternoons. As they stood in line for popcorn, Julie laughed suddenly and sharply.

"What's so funny?"

"I was thinking about the date. You know when he asked me if I liked Native or Indian."

"What did you say?"

"I asked him if he liked white or honky."

Nellie rolled her eyes as Julie doubled over at her own joke.

When they got home, Nellie checked the phone: *Ball, N.* had called. She showed it to Julie who shrugged and then turned on the TV. Nellie went back to her homework.

Homecoming

"COME HOME," HIS UNCLE said to him on the phone when Everett remembered to call one Christmas. Everett said that he would. So he did, a couple summers later. Just woke up one Friday, threw his bag in the truck and drove. He'd been down the road to the rez a few times before, hitting powwows here and there but not theirs. Never stopped in. *Because I've been there so many times before.* That must be it.

The yard was clean and neat and there were three cars parked there. He thought about turning around. They have visitors already. But that was stupid. He had to piss like a racehorse, anyways.

His uncle grinned when he saw him. "You look like you got rode hard and put away wet."

Everett chuckled. He saw who the third car was then. Eric, the older one, his arm around a brown haired girl and when she smiled up at Everett, he felt his pecker move. *Settle down, she's family.*

His aunt put some food in front of him and he sat down. He ate quietly while Eric told his dad about all the work he was doing at logging company out there in BC. He was working on "designing processes" which meant how things were done.

And he talked about management which Everett knew were the bosses. And he mentioned that they were having labour problems which Everett knew was him. And he grinned into his fried potatoes.

His uncle got up for more coffee. Everett noticed that his uncle had a gut that he hadn't had before. He asked Everett when he was getting new tires for his truck.

"Thought about it."

"Get 'em on." He growled. "Look like they haven't been changed since you took that truck." His uncle's truck was always gleaming. He would spend hours working on it, tightening this, replacing that, filling up fluid levels. Looked a lot like a job.

Eric turned the conversation back to him and to his girl. Her name was Sierra and in certain lights her eyes looked green. She was a photographer and worked for a production company out there in BC as an assistant producer.

Nope, Everett thought. *She gets coffee and her boss hits on her all the time.*

Eric asked Everett what he was doing and Everett described his last job which was cooking in a kitchen in Wanuskewin, this new cultural centre outside of Saskatoon. Even though cooking was really cutting things and mopping up late at night and smoking weed in the grass behind the Centre. He and his friends would make fun of the commercial for the place, "Come to Wanuskewin" some old guy in a thick accent would say. They would pretend to do the voice, drawling out: "Wanuskewin," trying to sound all Hollywood Indian.

"A cook?" his auntie repeated. She was at the counter, her hands in the sink washing up and he could see her shoulders shake.

"So you're Eric's brother?" Sierra said.

Everett and Eric spoke at the same time.

"I'm his cousin — "

"Kind of — "

"Raised together," his uncle said.

"Where are your parents?" She was one of those then. Not reserve raised so didn't know better than to ask questions like that.

Everett waited a second for someone else to speak and when they didn't, he said, "I never knew my dad, and my mom left me."

It sounded like a metal fork on a dish.

She exhaled a soft oh, then looked at Eric. Eric was looking at his watch. His uncle was staring at his smoke. That stupid "oh" wafted through the room like a fart.

"Left all of us." His auntie broke in, the door slamming shut on that subject.

∾ঔ∾ঔ∾ঔ

Everett followed his uncle around the yard. His uncle had built a firepit, a deck and was working on a new shed, even though he already had a few other sheds.

Everett ran his finger over the wood and talked about the construction details. His uncle didn't bite. Just handed him a hammer and put him to work.

A couple hours in, Eric and Sierra walked down the hill, his arm around her again. Everett smiled; his cousin was an idiot.

"Hey Dad, I'm gonna show Sierra around the rez."

"Be back for supper or your mom will be mad."

"Isn't Everett cooking us a five course meal?" Eric joked.

"Does it look like it?" his dad replied.

Eric looked at Everett who had lost track of what he was doing at least an hour ago. "You wanna come?"

Everett looked at his uncle. His uncle shrugged. "Let me change my shirt." Then he tried to remember if he had brought another one.

∾ᅌᅌ

Sierra told them that her production company was working on a documentary about an artist who grew up in Saskatchewan and painted pictures about life was he was young. She said the name and Everett was sure that he'd seen his pictures hanging in the halls of Wanuskewin.

"This is it, come to life," she said. "It's really beautiful."

"Nothing compared to BC." Eric said.

Everett hadn't been there yet but he agreed with Eric. Their rez was skinny bushes that you could see through in the winter (if they weren't covered with snow) and long grasses that hid wood-ticks, scratchy weeds and big rocks that tripped you.

"More houses now," Eric said.

"Why are they all the same?" Sierra asked.

"Indian affairs houses. Same kind of cheap house given to everyone. Same bad construction, same leaks, same mould problems."

Everett realized his cousin had been learning stuff then.

They passed a burnt-out building. Everett remembered it being a hall.

"Assholes," Eric said.

"I hope no one was hurt," Sierra said.

Everett could see how black the boards were and knew whoever set it meant for it burn to the ground. He'd seen guys that angry before. Saw them do things like punch through walls and shake their girlfriends until their teeth chattered. And when you tried to hold them down they'd throw you off and fight you like they wanted to kill you. Then the next day, they'd be the same nice guy you knew the day before. Life sure fucked with people.

They stopped at the store and picked up some cokes. Took a long time because everyone wanted to shake hands with Eric and Everett and ask them what they were up to and how come they didn't come by anymore. People looked shyly at Sierra but she boldly shook everyone's hands.

"Everyone likes you guys." Sierra held the seat so that Everett could jump in the back. "You're like the prodigal sons."

"You calling us fuck ups?" Eric asked.

"If the shoe fits." She was a tough one. That was good.

"Stop using such big words, Sierra. You're offending Everett."

"It's all good." Everett watched a group of young kids walking single file on the side of the road. One of them had a dog on a leash, that was a new one. Though when they drove past, he saw that it was only a piece of rope looped around the dog's neck.

"Let's go to the beach," Eric said.

It was a small lake, so small that you could canoe across it in less than an hour. But there was a bit of sand down there. They pulled up the car and walked close to the water. There were beer bottles and Eric picked up a few before giving up.

"Rubbies will get them," Everett reminded him.

Sierra took a deep breath. "Smells good."

Everett skipped a stone, it hit three times before sinking into the water. Eric picked up a few and Sierra asked him to show her how and soon they were on their own little date.

Everett remembered the last time he was here. He and Eric and Jason, and some other people were partying out there. Even though everyone was blasted, they were playing football half in the water, half out. Eric threw long and Everett dove for it. And hit one of those big old rocks hiding out there.

"You okay?" one of the girls had called out to him.

The world had been blurry. Everett remembered looking at the beach and it looked like there were hundreds standing there. Not the kids they were, but people from other times. And those old people were looking at him, like they could see him too. And even though he was standing up to his waist in water, he felt warm, like he was sitting by a wood fire.

He dragged his pounding head to the water's edge and dropped the football at his cousin Eric's feet. Someone tried to push a beer on him but he waved it off.

Everett had passed out on the beach and when he woke up everyone was gone. Probably someone's idea of a joke. The kind of joke Nellie would never laugh at. Everett chuckled, imagining her pissed off face.

"What are you laughing about?" Sierra asked.

"My girlfriend," he replied. Which he regretted a second after he said it.

"You have a girlfriend? Since when?" Eric was in his face.

"Since none of your business."

Eric pointed at Everett. "This guy was the biggest man-slut in our high school. Should've named an STD after him."

Sierra pursed her lips and turned away.

"What's her name?"

Eric knew the people on the rez even better than Everett did and there was only one Nellie. And if Eric knew he was dating Nellie then he would say something about her and Everett would have to punch him. Everett picked up another stone and skipped it.

"You forget her name?"

"Get out of my face." Everett said this under his breath to give Eric a chance before he kicked his ass in front of his girlfriend.

"I fucking knew it." Eric was walking back towards Sierra. "This guy — I knew he was lying. A tomcat will settle down before him."

Everett stared at his cousin and thought about telling them about that time they left him here with a concussion. But he kept his memory to himself along with the vision of the old people — which she probably would have liked. She was that kind of girl.

After supper, Everett walked out to his truck with his uncle.

"You need some money?"

Everett took the bills his uncle handed him.

"Take care of yourself."

"Yeah."

His uncle gave the truck another look over while Everett watched. Those questions that had been there since he was kid were bubbling up — that fucking Sierra girl — but he wasn't ready to hear the answers. So he sent his mind a few miles down the road, listening to tunes too loud with the window rolled down.

Friends

October 1995

"**W**HY IS *FRIENDS* ON every channel?" Everett asked from his permanent position on the couch. His ass had practically worn a dent in it.

Nellie ignored him as she addressed Julie. "I met the most annoying guy today." Julie wasn't listening. She was looking for her shoes in the shoebox.

Nellie hated the shoebox. It was such a rez thing. In the city people were supposed to organize their shoes on a shoe rack, not all scrambled together in an old microwave box. But she never managed to get around to buying a shoe rack and, more importantly, her budget didn't have room for decorative things.

Nellie turned her gaze towards Everett who was switching the TV over to the Nintendo. Nellie wasn't sure when he'd bought that when he told her all last week that he was too broke to do anything.

"First of all he came to the NSC meeting and he isn't even a member." Nellie was the secretary and treasurer on the Native Student Council. "He interrupted me twice and then he kept talking over me at the meeting." This was especially annoying because she barely spoke during meetings because she concentrated on taking completely accurate minutes. Also, she found that if she talked this only made meetings longer. So when she did have a point to make, it was an important one.

The president's name was Donna, she was a loud-mouthed native studies major who thought the annual student powwow was of paramount importance. Then there was Gordie, the vice president, who thought the annual student powwow was of even more paramount importance.There were a couple of other officers who never bothered to show up.

Meetings were generally short; Nellie scheduled half an hour for them in her planner. She thought the powwow was the least of their priorities. The Native students were facing cutbacks on their student funding thanks to Chretien. High rents were pushing students into bad areas and racist graffiti had popped up on school buildings. But arguing with those two assholes was a waste of time. Her student council experience would go on her resumé and resumé building was how Nellie would get to the next level — acceptance into law school, then work as a corporate lawyer in a good firm, then whatever else happened in life. Nellie wasn't sure what that was exactly but it probably involved having money for fancy shoe racks.

That afternoon, she was at the meeting, her pen poised for note-taking when the northerner walked in. You could always tell the northerners. They had black-black hair and pale skin like old-timey vampires and a cocky confidence that comes from isolation and not knowing any better.

"He's totally bush," Nellie said for the tenth time. "But he never shuts up. He thinks that every stupid idea that falls out of his mouth is a nugget of gold."

"You wanna bone him," Everett said.

"Gross, as if."

"Yup you got a crush."

"Not unless you mean crushing his big fat head in a vise." Nellie's tone was harsh but inside she was smiling that Everett showed a modicum of jealousy.

Nellie heard Julie laugh from the bottom of the shoe box. Then, "Where are my shoes?!" Julie was already late and getting later. Nellie couldn't figure out why Julie didn't lay out her outfit the night before work like she had suggested to her.

"And, he wouldn't shut up the whole meeting. He kept talking about organizing protests and lobbying for more funding — like we can even do that."

"I thought you wanted that too. Oh crap." Julie frowned as she bent over to pull a pair of boots on.

"What's wrong?" Everett asked.

"These boots have a heel and I hate wearing heels when I'm working."

"Puts a little junk in the trunk," Everett wound up as if to smack Julie in the ass. Nellie's eyes stopped him. He reached for the remote instead.

"You should tell him your ideas and then you two can work together and maybe even get rid those other two useless tits." Julie surveyed herself in the mirror by the door. Nellie had put it there after reading an article on good Feng Shui or maybe that was an article about being better organized?

Julie's collaboration/takeover idea had occurred to Nellie as well. During the meeting, she had noticed how the room crackled with energy when Taz entered it. And even though she found him ugly, he did have a strong voice and good posture. Nellie hated the way the other Native kids bent their heads and made their voices soft when they spoke, especially when they were around white people.

She wanted to smack them on the back of the head like the way her dad did when she was little. "Have some fucking pride," he would tell her and she would bite back tears but held her head up straight.

After the meeting, she'd been slow to pack up her stuff. Donna, of course, was hanging off of Taz. Donna went through men like a hot knife through lard. Nellie had to linger for a long time. She packed and unpacked her backpack a couple times before Donna scuttled off to go make supper for her kids. Nellie glanced at him from beneath her hair. He was studying the giant map of Indian reserves of Saskatchewan hanging on the wall. Students placed pins in their home communities.

He said something in Cree. Nellie asked, "What?"

"Where are you from?" He asked glancing at her but not turning around.

"Stone Man's."

"Asinîy napew."

"Yes that's how we say it in Cree."

"Why don't you speak your language?"

"My parents didn't teach us."

"There's classes here."

Nellie knew that but she didn't dare take one. Language classes were hard to score high marks in and she didn't want a low grade bringing her average down.

"Don't you think it's important for First Nations people to know their own language?" His tone suggested that he was working his way up to a speech.

"It doesn't make me Native."

"Doesn't it? It's a connection to our past. Like the drum."

"There are other connections."

Taz held his hands out as if to say, "Enlighten me!" Nellie laughed sharply to cover her anger and then said she had to go — and she did have to go, she had a class starting in ten minutes.

Taz laughed then and Nellie knew it was at her. She tried not to look like she was scurrying out the door.

"Why should I work with him? I've been a member of the council for two years and I know those two morons aren't capable of taking a shit without asking an Elder for permission first.I know that but who's he to question them?"

"What's his name?" Everett asked.

"I told you. His name is Nathan. Nathan Mosquito. But he prefers 'Taz' — how fucking stupid is that? And I don't know which reserve he's from, but he's definitely some dumbass bush Indian."

Everett looked towards the ceiling. This meant he was thinking. "Does he have a dimple chin?"

"Yeah."

"I know that guy."

"What?"

Julie slipped out the door and called out "bye" over her shoulder.

"Bye Jules!" Everett called back.

"You know him? How do you know him?" Nellie moved to stand over Everett, blocking his view of the TV, which was the best way to keep his attention.

"I met him when I was working at that moving company. Y'know the one that paid by the pallet? What a rip off that was. Do you know how much shit people can load on a single pallet? If I hadn't been stealing that guy blind, I would've been pissed."

Nellie stifled a sigh and kept her voice light. "So he was working there?"

"No, Officer. I know him because he buys drugs from my roommate."

"Oh." Nellie felt better. A stupid pothead was no competition. "Wait, you're living with a drug dealer?"

⋖⋗⋖⋗⋖⋗

Julie wasn't home the next morning. It was Shaylene that noticed. "Julie's not home," she said to Nellie who stood in front of the fridge trying to figure out what to make for breakfast.

Nellie felt that familiar twinge of envy when someone else was having an exciting life — even though Everett, the love of her life, was in her bedroom lying spread-eagled across her star quilt. From the kitchen, she could even hear him farting. Envy was just her knee-jerk response to all things Julie.

"She's a big girl." Nellie pulled out the frying pan. She was going to make the perfect breakfast. Bacon and eggs for her man. She made a face at that phrase — it sounded so archaic, so rez. She shrugged. *It was true.*

"I wanted to pay her the money I owe her," Shaylene said.

"She lent you money?" Nobody ever lent Nellie money; not that she ever asked.

"I'm going to leave it here," Shaylene tucked it under the couch.

"Why don't you wait? She'll be home soon I'm sure."

"I might forget."

Nellie rolled her eyes at that, how many things could Shaylene have on her plate? She never went anywhere. "Want some breakfast?"

Shaylene nodded but walked back to her bedroom.

Nellie had wanted to chitchat. She felt like stuff was starting to happen between her and Everett. Like when she was describing a paper she was writing, it seemed like he was listening and that night he had kept one arm around her, most of the night

Now, when she talked to her mom on Sunday, she could tell her that "her boyfriend" might be coming down for Christmas and that they should make sure to get some beer because her "boyfriend" liked to drink. Or maybe they didn't have to get any beer at all because maybe he wouldn't want to drink when his friends weren't around?

Her mom had already told Nellie that she thought Everett drank too much.

Nellie tried to explain the way she saw it in her head. "It's not a big deal because I like to drink too. We're a couple that likes to drink like Liz Taylor and what's-his-name. Once he gets a good job and I graduate, we'll slow down, like how people do."

Her mom dropped it but Nellie knew it was being discussed around the dinner table. "Nellie's got a guy but he's trouble." Her mom would suggest a visit and her dad would say he was too busy. Her sister would gossip and Nellie would get teased about it when she went home.

As long she kept bringing in good marks, she didn't see how her life was anyone's business.

"Eggs are burning," Everett walked past her directly to the living room. He fell on the couch with a dull thud and clicked on the TV.

If she tried, she could probably get him to take her to a movie in the afternoon. She was pretty sure he had money, he'd only gotten paid on Wednesday and even though he went out that night, not even Everett could spend his whole paycheque in one night. *Could he?* Nellie felt tired suddenly.

"Serve yourself," she called to the living room. "I feel sick."

"What?"

Nellie turned off the stove and walked back towards her bedroom like a dog on the scent of rotting meat.

Nellie was lying in bed when Julie got in. She heard the door shut and the sound of voices. She recognized Everett's joking tones and Julie's laugh ring out. He was probably teasing her about staying out all night. Then Nellie heard another voice. Deeper than Julie's and loud. Very loud.

Nellie popped out of the room. She saw Taz and he turned and saw her. "Hi!" He called down the hallway. Nellie closed her bedroom door. She looked in her mirror. Her hair was crazy. She pulled it back in a ponytail and replaced her baggy pajama pants with jeans.

She curled herself around the corner of the living room. Everett was sitting on the couch. Julie leaned against the wall and Taz sat in the easy-chair looking like he belonged there.

Nellie couldn't take her eyes off of Julie's smile. Happy and lopsided. Her eyes were tired but shiny. Nellie looked at Taz, he was talking, of course. Practically yelling some story about a fight he almost got into the night before. He talked fast too, leaping over multiple ideas in a single bound. He had a dozen voices as he acted out characters; he was a one-man conversation band.

Not him, Nellie thought. *Why did it have to be him?*

"We're going out for breakfast!" Julie told Nellie. "Grab your jacket."

"And comb your hair," Taz added.

"It's the afternoon."

"It is?" Julie giggled.

"So what? Denny's serves breakfast all day."

Nellie glanced at the guy she slept with otherwise known as her boyfriend. "Everett?"

Everett shrugged.

Nellie brightened a bit. He wouldn't have said yes if he didn't have a little bit of money.

"We should bring Shay," Nellie said, mostly because Shaylene would say something if she wasn't at least asked even though she wouldn't go anyway.

Nellie hurried down the hallway and knocked on her door. Sometimes Shaylene wore headphones and listened to music while she studied even though Nellie had explained to her that it took extra energy for the brain to drown out the music to focus on her work. Nellie pushed the door open.

Later she said that the room felt thick and silent.

Nellie headed towards the bed and laid her hand on the blanketed body there. Shaylene's eyes were closed. Nellie shook her and said her name. Nellie shook harder and there was a heaviness to her body that was wrong.

She called her name this time.

Nellie picked up Shaylene's wrist for a pulse. She'd always been good at that in first aid classes, somebody would say that they couldn't find a pulse and Nellie would grab their wrist and find it in under ten seconds. Every time. She was pretty sure it was some kind of gift. Nellie dropped her hand and hesitated: 911 or compressions — which which which . . .

Her eyes spotted the phone next to the mattress. Much later this would be a detail that would make Nellie hold a pillow to her mouth and scream. She dialled quickly. Words tumbled out. Then Nellie began to push on her chest, one hand over the other, like she'd been taught. Julie was the first to find her; she called the guys to help. One of them took over. Nellie waited patiently for her turn.

Later the girls sat on the couch together. The paramedics had wrapped them in these metal looking blankets. Nellie always remembered how kind they were.

When she could speak, she told Julie that Shaylene had left some money for her under the couch. Julie nodded but Nellie could tell she hadn't heard her. Nellie reached for it, wanting to know for sure that it was gone.

Taz and Everett walked in together, they'd followed the paramedics to the ambulance.

"Where's the money?" Nellie stared at Everett.

"What money?"

"The money she left for Julie. She put it under the couch."

"I didn't know." He rummaged through his pockets and put it in Julie's lap. Julie didn't seem to notice.

Everett went to sit next to Nellie and put his arm around her. She pushed his arm away.

Nellie felt her mind making lists, then un-making them. She could feel sentences floating through her mind, out of order. She had nothing to grab on to.

"You aren't making any sense," Everett told her. He called her mom.

"We're coming to get you," her mom's voice was warm and solid.

"Julie too."

"Of course."

Nellie held the phone in her hand after she hung up. She ran through her lists and came up empty. *Nothing can make me happy.*

Taz gave them tea. Nellie would always remember that.

New Year's Eve

1996

TAZ BLACKED OUT A lot. So much that he even had an after-blackout routine. He would wake up the next morning and tell everyone that he got fucked up, make some jokes about what an idiot he was and then buy everyone breakfast.

Things he did not remember:

1. Shooting his uncle's rifle at an outhouse. And missing like four times. He never understood why no one took the rifle away from him. He imagined that his cousins and uncle and other dumbassed family members stood there laughing at him as he shot at it. They said he kept yelling about a bear.

2. Eating dog food like it was cereal. It wasn't the worst thing someone could do but it felt weird to stare at the bag on the table the next afternoon and the bowl of milky pink substance next to it and realize that someone had done that and that his swollen gut said it was him.

3. Puking all over his bed and waking up with his face in it. During the shower and laundry day that followed, he had a long time to think about how close he had come to death.

4. Driving himself home. Too many times to count. Waking up in bed and not knowing how he got there. Like at all. His jacket and shoes pooled beside his bed, his keys on the bedside table. He always felt a frisson of pride, his blackout self rocked.

5. Passing out in strange places: a closet, under a bed, in a chicken coop, behind the high school dumpster, near the train tracks, half in and half out of a pond.

No matter what he did, other than teasing him, nobody ever sat him down and said, "Taz, you have a problem."

He found out after he started drinking that people let things slide when you were drunk. Live and let live, that was the code. He might yell at his friends and call them dumb fucks or tell his girlfriend that she was a slut or stand toe to toe with his dad and call him a fucking loser to his face but not a single one of them ever confronted him afterwards.

His friends might be a bit crusty for a few days after, his girlfriend might not kiss him the same way and his dad might not meet his eyes anymore, but those were tiny consequences like a single bruise after falling down a set of stairs.

Most of this stuff happened up north in Crow's Nest where he grew up and he figured that once he got to the city, he would leave it all behind.

In the city, he wouldn't drink like that anymore because he would be busy with school and work and making connections; he would be building things, not tearing them apart. Crow's Nest was behind him along with all of his sad eyed friends and their growing guts and whining that the chief and council sucked but never doing anything about it.

The day before he left, he went moose hunting with his best friend Travis. Travis had a girlfriend who was pregnant and

Travis, dumb fuck, was hoping for twins. All the way into the woods, he kept talking about how lucky twins were and how they ran in both his and his girlfriend's families. Every word out of his mouth drove home why Taz needed to get the fuck out of there.

They got into a good spot and made a few moose calls. Travis could do a cow so good that if he closed his eyes, he'd think she was standing right next to him. With a guy like that you weren't wasting your time.

"How you gonna live without all this?" Travis asked as they lay on their sides splitting a smoke. Taz had a tree root right under his hip but at least the ground wasn't wet. He inhaled the scent of the fir tree and felt it move down into the bottom of his lungs.

"Can't stay here forever."

"You could run for chief. I'd support you."

"Not yet." And probably, not ever. Being chief of Crow's Nest might be something to most people on the rez but not Taz.

He'd been a few times to the city and came home feeling something. That was enough for him.

"Lots of girls gonna be disappointed. Falen for sure."

"She's got future Marineland written all over her."

"Aw, c'mon she's fucking hot."

"Give her two years. Only place she ever wanted me to take her was KFC."

"You're really gonna leave all of this?"

"Like I'm Ben Johnson on steroids."

"Run Forrest, run."

They shot a bull and butchered it in the woods. It took longer than Taz expected. They thought about hanging out in the woods overnight but Travis decided that his girlfriend might get worried and call the cops or something. So they wrapped up the meat and hiked out.

"It's not gonna be the same without you Taz."

Taz grunted. The cold was moving in on them, creeping in through the cracks in their clothing. Taz liked how it felt, how it made him feel awake.

He figured once he got away from Crow's Nest, he would be all business. Let the fuckers up there barbecue and social their life away, he was going to do something with his life.

But the people in the city turned out to be exactly like the people on the rez. There was always another party, another reason to turn it up.

The first one to five drinks, he was grinning and all of his worries drifted away. Sometimes that feeling was still there when he woke up, lingering on the edges of his consciousness. Then *bam*, regrets hit him. Best thing to do in that situation was to go for a run and tell himself all over again, that he was done. No more drinking.

That's what he did his first New Year's Day in Saskatoon. After his First New Year's Eve, with Julie.

That morning started slow. Nellie had spent it nagging Julie to try on dresses. Nellie wanted them to go all out, all dressed up, but even though Julie was nodding her head, Taz knew she wouldn't do it. Julie hated dresses. She thought they were too cold, too girlie and too dumb.

Plus Taz wasn't going out with her looking like that. He already had to deal with all the sharks circling her. No need to throw chum in the water. He only had two fists.

Nellie told Everett he had to get the tickets for the social at the bar.

"It's the only thing you have to do today." She said it with a tight, sad smile that reminded Taz of his mother. Why did they always set themselves up for disappointment?

Taz knew getting the tickets was his job. Julie sat at the table with her head in her hands. She had a headache from doing shots the night before. Taz had goaded her into them, saying he wanted to see her drunk. So she got drunk, turned out she was exactly the same: quiet.

He didn't get her at all. But at least nobody else could either.

Sometimes he got glimpses of who she was. They would be arguing and suddenly she'd start crying and Taz would realize he'd hit something. Then he'd backtrack and try to figure out what it was. Because you could yell at her and call her a dozen names and she wouldn't show any reaction.

She never cried very long and she liked to do it in private. She'd run away from him, as far and as long as it would take to make sure he couldn't see her do it. And if he held her down she would cry silently with her eyes closed.

It wasn't like he wanted to see her cry, he just liked knowing that she felt things.

If she's with you, then she wants to be there. That's what he told himself. For whatever reason, she had chosen the short guy over the tall guys, the poor student over the rich dudes, the Indian guy over the white guys that were always sniffing around.

He wasn't going to second guess it even though the doubts crawled all over him at night. Sometimes when they had sex no matter how deep inside of her he was he felt like it wasn't enough. He wanted her so much and he knew she would never want him that much. Nobody could.

He still remembered the first time he saw her, leaning against the bar. The douchebag bartender was trying to talk to her but her eyes were on the crowd. She seemed to be staring at something but that was a trick she did. She was rarely looking at anything.

He thought she had to be someone's girlfriend until he saw her tray.

She was a shitty waitress but nobody seemed to mind. She went to tables when she felt like it and the guys tried to hold her there as long as possible. The girls at the table tried to chase her away with quick drink orders or else they wanted her to stay and talk her ear off, wanted to know her secrets for being so pretty. She looked tired.

Taz wasn't someone who asked out women. They sort of came to him around 2:00 AM when they realized that he was the guy who bought the shots and chose the party.

He knew she would never come to him as soon as he saw her. So he walked across the dance floor. He started walking before he even decided to do it. Like time travelling backwards.

And then she said yes to whatever he asked her and after her shift they went drinking together. Her hand felt smooth and cold in his. She was fucking tall though and if he was straight with himself, she was as tall as he was.

"You're a goddamn giraffe," he told her.

She laughed and punched him in the kidney.

They ran into a bunch of people he knew and they drank and bullshitted for hours. His eyes kept going to her. Usually she was staring at something else but once in a while his eyes would meet her and he would feel a jolt and feel scared for a second. Then he'd push that away because he wasn't a chickenshit. She was just a girl.

They were always together after that except that time she had gone away to her rez for a week and he followed her a few days into it. He had classes but he didn't care. He had this feeling that if he wasn't there something would happen. She wasn't the cheater type but he knew guys, they would do anything. Or, what if she was in a car with an idiot driving too fast? Car accidents happened all the time. And none of those rez houses had carbon monoxide detectors or too many of them had wood stoves and who knew what could happen? So he went and she was happy to see him.

He could see into the future with her. He saw their kids, their house, her getting older but still staying pretty. He told her about it one time when he was drunk and she laughed and looked away which made him crazy. But she stayed with him so he figured he had a chance. He tried not to say stupid things like that again.

Taz gave her a kiss as he and Everett left the apartment that afternoon. First they went to wash Taz's car. Then, Everett took him to his dealer's house and they bought some weed and Taz splurged on some coke.

Even though he was a poor student, his dad sent him money every once in a while and his band asked him to do stuff for them. Just paperwork and running around the city. He wasn't a bum like Everett. Not that Everett had to be a bum, the dude knew enough about construction that he could get his journeyman and make lots of money but he wasn't interested. Taz told him all the time how stupid and lazy he was. Everett laughed it off.

"You don't know what's really important," Everett would tell him, as if he had it all figured out. Everett had that whole fucking house to himself so he didn't understand what everyone else was dealing with.

Taz had moved Nellie and Julie into his apartment. They didn't want to go back to their place after that girl died there. He didn't want Nellie to move in but of course Julie wouldn't go without her. Nellie was okay but he hated the way she watched everything like a goddamn spy. He left the toilet seat up and she was the first one to complain. He raised his voice and her lips pinched together. He had a beer and she started counting. He couldn't even be himself in his own place. He wished that Everett would move her in — even told him to — but Everett just laughed.

Nellie had a hard-on for that dipshit that bordered on obsession. She was a smart enough chick but not smart enough to know that she should be with someone more like her. She clung to Everett like a kid with her red balloon.

Being with Julie made living with Nellie easier to bear. She came home and laid down on top of him, smelling like smokes, booze and hairspray, and he never smelled anything so good in his life. They would melt together until Nellie came in and planted herself on the other chair, not looking at them but very much watching them.

Taz and Everett stayed long at the dealer's house because Everett was trying to get some mushrooms out of the guy for free. Everett would fuck a dead horse if he thought there was something in it for him. He was always telling Taz that money didn't matter. And yet the guy was always desperate for it like a junkie. It flowed through him and Taz wondered if Nellie knew what she was getting herself into.

The dealer had this seventeen-year-old cousin who took a liking to Everett so then he had to fuck her in the bathroom. The dealer turned up the music to drown out the sound. The girl was pudgy in the middle with angry pimples across her chin; even Nellie was hotter than this pork rind. Taz couldn't figure out why Everett would waste his time but Everett was like that. Part of his free life philosophy or something.

Taz had been free his whole life and didn't see the fucking thrill. Being tied to something, having people depend on him, wanting to be him, that's where the real thrill was. Having people wait on the precipice for his decision, that was power.

People were already asking him to run for grand chief of the Assembly of Saskatchewan Chiefs. He always looked them in the eye and looked for their underneath thoughts. He was good at that. "There's always another level," his dad used to tell him. They might be encouraging him to run but only to find out what his ambitions were and how they might exploit them.

Taz's dad had made it to chief of his reserve that only had five hundred members. But that didn't stop Old Sam from talking a big game over beers at the dinner table. "You come from chiefs, you're a chief," he would tell Taz, sometimes in a proud voice, sometimes angry, sometimes with tears making rivulets down his pockmarked skin.

Then Sam would break out the stories. Some of them were self-pitying tripe about how people were never grateful and how even your best friends would fuck you over if push came to shove.

But others were about strategy, like about how to make them want the same things you did and make them think that it was their idea all along.

And then other stories about when to stand firm, when to compromise, when to bitch-slap motherfuckers until they towed the line. Taz listened to them all.

Taz figured his dad could have had it all. But too many nights sitting at the table until five in the morning, Sam would blame it on twenty different things. Taz hated that weak shit. Nothing and nobody could stop you, if you really wanted something.

Everett finished with the girl and they went out to the car. It was five and already fucking cold. The cut off for the tickets was at six. Taz raced across town while Everett described this spot on the girl's vagina that had felt like a tongue.

"It was like rubbing on my dick. Drove me crazy."

"Herpes."

"Nah, shit, it wasn't that."

"It was fucking herpes."

"Fuck don't tell me that. I gotta act straight."

"Shut up for a second then."

"Did you do that coke?"

"No. And don't ask 'cause I'm not sharing it."

"Nah, fuck, I already took something. That girl had some acid."

"That was dumb."

"I know right. I'm not even sure why I—" He stopped.

Taz looked over and Everett was staring at the ceiling.

He drove on and hoped that no cop would pull up beside them and see the dumb Indian staring up at the ceiling like a dead person.

He pulled up at the bar and ran in for the tickets. He didn't want to go to the bar at all but he had to make an appearance. He had to get out there and buy drinks and punch fists and be that guy.

Then he filled up the car and headed home. As he was pulling up in front of the building he looked over at Everett. "Wake up, fuck-face."

Everett was staring at his hands. "There's spiders on the mattress. Where's the flyswatter?"

"Get out of the car."

Everett nodded. But then instead of opening his car door, he climbed through the middle of the two front seats and slumped across the backseat. He was combing over the car seats with his hands. "Lots of spiders."

"None of that shit. We're home. Get the fuck inside."

"Do you know that spiders kill fifteen thousand children a year? I read that."

"You don't know how to read, you fucking moron."

Everett started to laugh. His shoulders moved up and down and he shook but no sound came out.

Taz slammed the door and headed inside. He didn't know much about acid but Everett did. He should, he chewed through everything like a garbage disposal. Everett even tried dealing for a while — which was how they met in the first place but he couldn't sell right. He gave stuff away or smoked it all up or lost it. He was probably the worst drug dealer the city had ever seen. He actually failed at being a drug dealer. That never failed to amaze Taz.

Taz opened the door and heard music. The girls were in the bedroom when he got in. He pulled a beer from the fridge and cracked it, loving that sound. He pounded it back.

Nellie turned the corner, "Where's Everett?"

"Outside."

"How cold is it?"

"Cold." *If a northerner said it was cold, it was fucking cold.*

"I'm not wearing a dress," Julie yelled from the bedroom. "I'm not freezing my ass off."

Nellie rolled her eyes and reached past Taz for a beer. "Nobody ever wants to celebrate anything. Did you get the tickets?"

Taz nodded.

"I can't believe this. The first time I'm going out on New Year's Eve."

"That's fucking sad." Taz tossed the tickets on the table.

Julie peeked her head around the corner. "Hey," she said breathlessly.

Taz grabbed her wrist and pulled her towards him. She had on a grey-blue strapless dress. It was made for a girl Nellie's size so on Julie, the skirt ended half way on her thighs making her legs go on forever.

"What do you think?"

"You look like a whale."

Julie laughed.

Nellie slapped him in the gut. "What the fuck? Nobody is skinnier than Julie."

"I mean the colour of them."

"Nah, you think I'm Orca. I get it. He thinks I'm a killer whale." Julie took a sip of his beer.

It's scary how good you look.

Those words would never come out of his mouth. He took a sip of beer and kissed her right in front of Nellie.

Taz had never been to the ocean but that's what kissing Julie felt like.

He pulled her against him. She was so tall that it was awkward to rest his chin on her shoulder.

"Where's Everett?" Nellie was looking at the door.

"Outside I told you."

"Is he coming in?"

"I don't know why he's out there in the first place."

Nellie sighed and went to the door. She piled on her jacket-boots-scarf-gloves and went outside.

Julie kissed him again and he lost track of time. He came up for air to shoot back another beer.

"You better start drinking, you're already two behind," he told her.

Julie made a face. "I only stopped throwing up like an hour ago."

Taz went to the bathroom. He took the mirror the girls used to pluck their eyebrows and made a line on it with the coke. It was a small line. He snorted. Felt like a nose-ful of angry pepper. He took a sip of beer. Balanced.

He went back to the living room. Julie joined him on the couch. She had changed back into her usual jeans and sweat-shirt combo. He nuzzled her neck and wished that they lived alone especially as Nellie tramped inside. She slammed the door.

"What is he on?" she demanded of Taz.

Taz shrugged. "Just relax Nellie."

"He's acting like a fucking lunatic." She stood there in her tights and snow boots and dress and Taz felt sorry for her.

"Normal for him." Taz laughed and Julie giggled into his shoulder.

"Maybe we should take him to the hospital?"

"As if." She was such a bonehead. He'd wrestle the keys away from her before he'd let that happen. Go to the police and she'd get the whole bunch of them thrown in jail for the weekend. She had a room full of books and was still a moron.

The door opened behind her. Everett peeked around the corner. Nellie peppered him with questions that he wouldn't or probably couldn't answer.

Taz turned on the TV. This wasn't his problem. He flipped through the channels. Sometimes the States played some good concerts before midnight.

Everett moved to a chair at the table and looked halfway decent, though his eyes were dilated. Nellie stared at him; she'd run out things to say.

"Have a beer, Nellie," Taz called from the living room. "You look too sober."

When she turned to him, he could see her mouth trembling like a sick dog. But she went to the fridge and Taz heard the opening of a beer.

Everett said something, kind of sharp so Taz looked at him. He was mumbling and slowly building volume. Taz realized he was singing. Taz turned down the TV. It took a few seconds for him to recognize the song, "All My Ex's Live in Texas". All three of them turned their attention to him. Everett kept singing, confidently like he was a cabaret performer. Julie started clapping along. Taz glanced at Nellie, she looked as shocked as he felt. The song got loud enough for the neighbours to knock on the wall — Taz thought he was nailing it.

"Way to go Everett" Taz yelled. And Everett stood up and sang the last note, more like a shout than a song at that point. "Hang my head in Tennessee!"

Taz jumped up to shake his hand. "Where'd you learn that? Your dad?"

Taz thought that was a fair question so he was surprised when Everett swung at him. Everett was a big guy, long-armed like a chimp so even though Taz ducked, the edge of his fist still connected to the side of his head. "You motherfuck-" Taz had to duck another punch.

Nellie jumped in and grabbed Everett's arm. She hung off it like a cat. Taz grabbed at his other so between the two them they wrestled him back into the seat.

"What the hell, man?" Taz asked. He was breathless and his ears were still ringing. He wanted to slug the stupid look off Everett's face but that lunkhead was laughing now. Taz looked at Nellie. She was shaking her head, fretting away with her fingers in her mouth.

It was Julie who said from behind him, her hand on his arm. "We should go."

But first, I'm going to fucking kill this guy. Everett was drinking out of the beer Nellie had handed him. The liquid was dribbling out of the side of his mouth. Taz let Julie pull him away.

"It's getting late already." Her voice was in his ear, the one that was growing hot from where he'd been hit.

"Better call for a cab then."

"I can drive," Julie said.

"No, you're drinking." This was an order. He didn't want her standing near the door all night trying to go home.

"She should drive," Nellie disagreed, "or we're gonna be waiting for cabs all night."

"Let's play poker!" Everett said, his head on the kitchen table now like he was trying to pass out.

"Nobody's playing. And take your fucking shoes off, you're making the floor wet." Taz snatched his beer off the table. Too bad it was illegal to beat up the mentally handicapped.

They played quarter bounce until the cab came. Everyone drank but Nellie probably the most. She had a determined look on her face as she stared at Everett across the table.

Taz went to the bathroom one more time before they left. He had a long night of fistbumping in front of him and wanted to have enough energy to do it.

The bar was a trip. Some dude dressed up as the year 1996 and everyone took turns slapping and kicking him at him on the dance floor. "Die, die, die!" they chanted and everyone laughed.

"5–4–3–2 . . ."

Taz and Julie danced to "Auld Lang Syne" which he had never figured out. "Nellie's crying in the bathroom," Julie whispered in his ear, "because she can't find Everett." He ignored that. They weren't his problem.

He felt like there were people cheering. Why were they cheering?

"4–3–2 . . ." Taz found himself taking a swing at a guy. Guy was a lot bigger and Taz's fist bounced off his chin and drunk as he was, he could feel a stinging in his wrist.

"There'll be times when you only get one swing," his dad's voice cautioned. Taz saw the next fist before it hit him. He smelled, then tasted the blood. It shot directly to the back of his throat and he choked a little. He threw another fist as he went down.

All the way down. Feet. Lots of girls wearing high heels — *in the middle of fucking winter? What the fuck.*

Then lower. He couldn't see nothing, he could barely hear. "Julie?"

Stairs. They were carrying him out. The snow was fucking cold. They stood him up and he felt sick. He was going to be sick. He put his head down and saw all the blood in the snow. There was a hand on his waist, then, "Oh, Taz."

Why were people laughing? What were they laughing at? He wasn't the person to laugh at. He started swinging again and when his fist connected, it didn't feel right.

1 . . .

He woke up. The sun was streaming in because someone had torn the curtains down. One clung to the corner of the rod. Taz reached across the bed, the mattress felt cold. There were footsteps in the hall. He tried his voice. It was too dry and it took much effort. A woman was crying.

He followed the sound because on the other side of it was the kitchen where there was water and for God's sake he might be dying but he wanted water first. He struggled to his feet and used the wall for support.

He called for Julie and hated the sound of his voice, raspy and weak. He opened the door and saw the girls on the floor. He couldn't tell who was comforting who until they lifted their heads. Nellie's face was wet with tears and red-tinged. He kept walking past.

He drank water and felt like it was a food, the most filling food he'd ever eaten. He stayed in the kitchen for a long time, waiting for the tableau around the corner to resolve itself. He heard them murmuring. The pronoun "he" kept coming up. That had to be Everett — where was he? That must be the reason for the tears. "Mexico" that was that student placement that Nellie had been offered. She was leaving then?

He didn't want to get his hopes up. He clenched his fist and noticed his knuckles were swollen and there was blood on his high school class ring. He went to the freezer and pushed his hand inside. He held it in the cold next to the vanilla ice cream. Why did everything have to hurt twice as bad when you were sober? Why couldn't you feel some of it when you were drunk? Beause maybe that would stop you.

He stumbled to the bedroom and fell asleep again.

When he woke, Julie was lying next to him. Her eyes were on his face. He could see a bruise and a scratch by her left eye but it was far up by her temple; her hair could cover it. He closed his eyes again.

"What do you remember from last night?" she asked. Her voice was like a rabbit's footprints on new snow.

She fell asleep waiting for his answer.

The Resistance

May 1997

NELLIE WALKED THROUGH THE automatic doors and was hit full in the face with a draft of hot wind. She staggered; the difference was so extreme.

She stopped to catch her breath and look around. Everyone was greeting family and friends and not paying any attention to her. She was grateful for that. She pulled a worn itinerary from her purse and unfolded it. "Station four," she said through parched lips, "Four PM." She had no idea what time it was and attempted to do the math in her tired brain — why couldn't she sleep on planes? (*Because I need to be awake to keep the plane in the air through my will alone.*)

She left Saskatoon at 6:00 AM. She stood in line next to her mom, Natalie, who was sipping a coffee and giving her tips about surviving in Central America even though she'd never left Saskatchewan herself. "You can't drink the water, no matter how much they want you to. You know, the Queen only travels with her own water — "

"How is that remotely relevant?"

" — and if someone tries to sell you something, never take the first price, always ask for less. It's rude if you *don't* haggle. And, snakes — there are lots of snakes — make sure you always wear long socks."

"I'm not wearing socks in thirty degree weather."

"And don't forget to enjoy yourself, you earned it. You got into into law school." Natalie said this loudly — so that everyone within a half mile distance could hear.

Nellie cringed. "Geez, Mom." And then bent her head so that her mom could kiss her forehead.

Nellie got through security and on the plane and sat there staring ahead at the seat until it was time to change planes in Toronto. Then an even longer flight, spent leafing through fashion magazines and not thinking about Everett and what a fucking asshole he was and how come he didn't even come see her at the airport? And then landing and looking out the window, and seeing green jungle on both sides of the airstrip and realizing, "Holy shit, what have I done?"

Green. Nellie had only seen that kind of green on the hills near Lebret though you could live in Lebret a thousand years and it would never get this hot. She spotted a store across the street — there would be beer there. She checked both ways before crossing — was that a donkey driving a cart? What the fuck? Maybe she should have researched Mexico before she flew there. Nellie never did things blindly but then again she'd never broken up with the love of her life before. The last four months were a blur of papers, exams, law school applications and filling out paperwork for the trip.

Julie had tried to talk her out of it a few times, "Next year we can do a spring break trip, Taz said he'll pay for it." (Taz had gotten hired at the Assembly of Saskatchewan Chiefs as some kind of policy analyst.) But Nellie didn't want a trip; she wanted to be away from everything that reminded her of Everett.

The sun beat down on her. She should have chugged water on the plane like her mom suggested. Every step felt like she was walking through a fog of someone's sweat, but she kept walking until she got inside the store. She expected/hoped to feel a blast of AC. It was hotter in the store. She made eye contact with the man behind the counter — he looked like the guys back home on her rez — and he nodded. She nodded back and walked to the back of the store. She found a beer fridge and leaned her forehead against it. "I can do this." She whispered. Then she slid the fridge door open and pulled out a beer.

She took her time walking outside to waiting area four. By the time she got there, there was a group of people waiting there. All white, all blonde, all skinny. It was like her worst nightmare had followed her from Saskatchewan.

"*Buenos dias,*" this from a tall blond guy, his long curly hair twisted into dreads.

"Yeah, thanks." Nellie sipped her beer and wished that everyone would stop looking at her.

The guy laughed. "I thought you were a local!" He turned to the group behind him, lounging on the bench and their suitcases. "I thought she was a local."

A couple of blonde girls looked Nellie up and down, and then looked away, bored already.

"Where did you get that?" asked dreadlocks, his eyes on her beer.

Nellie pointed at the convenience store directly across from the tiny airport.

He hesitated. "I wonder if I should . . . "

"Should what?" Nellie asked. Talk to the locals? Weren't they here to work with people?

"It's just that this is a Christian organization and drinking is . . . frowned upon."

Nellie took another sip. "Didn't know that," she said casually even as her heart was sinking. *And that is why you read shit thoroughly and don't jump blindly into situations.*

When the bus came, Nellie got on last, careful to stow her empty beer in her bag lest someone get mad at her for destroying the environment by leaving it behind. *And late at night I can sniff it and remember what life was like.*

When they were all on, the bus driver stood up and addressed them. His name was Marcos and he was short (like everyone Nellie had seen so far) but also handsome with dark eyes, dark skin and black hair. Kind of like a Native guy but different. He asked for everyone's names and how much Spanish they knew. The blonde girls who looked like twins were Margot and Melanie, they had just met on the plane but looked like they were already best friends — they even wore the same layered tanktops and linen pants. The "M"s, Nellie stored in her head. Dreadlocks was Noah. There was a tall, blonde girl with short hair who looked exactly like the model Linda Evangelista. Her name was Nicole. Then there were two clean-cut looking dudes, like the kind of guys who ran for student government and always won. They were something and something. Nellie had lost focus by them, starting to feel the effects of an early morning flight and the heat. Everyone spoke some Spanish.

"You?" Marcos leaned in so he could see her back there in the shadows.

"Nellie."

"Neelee." He hit the "e's" pretty hard. "What does it mean?"

"I think I was named after my mom's horse."

Marcos threw back his head and laughed like a Native person.

"*Habla espanol?*"

Nellie shook her head. "Just "*hola*" and "*si*" and . . . " she was gonna say cerveza but decided against it.

Marcos smiled, "Sometimes yes is all you need."

He explained that everyone would be staying with families in the same village. They were expected to meet every morning for work assignments. He was sort of vague about what that would be.

"For the church, right?" Nicole asked.

"I thought it was a school!" Nellie blurted out. That was the picture that had attracted Nellie. She kind of liked the idea of helping poor kids get an education and become rich and powerful — although that hadn't happened to her yet.

"Kind of both," Marcos said, and climbed back into the driver's seat.

The village was named Gutierrez and it was bigger than Nellie had figured. The streets were a mix of dirt and not dirt — she thought she even heard some cobblestone under the van. The buildings were low like thrown together buildings with lots of advertisements on the front and others were old and noble looking. Or at least what she could see, it had gone dark like someone had turned out the light. Fantastic burning sun and then — nothing. She kept yawning at the back of the bus and wondered how the rest of them could be so chatty.

Marcos dropped them off in twos. The "M"s went first. Then Nicole and Noah. Then the two future conservative-party-members. Outside each house a man and woman and a few children would greet the young people and wave to Marcos.

This is the real deal, Nellie thought. Marcos kept driving on and Nellie realized that she was the last one on the bus. Seventh is the unluckiest number she thought and wondered for the first time how she was going to survive on her own.

Marcos turned up the hill and drove around a winding drive. It was a lot further than the other places so Nellie walked up to his seat. "Did you forget about me?" she asked.

He said nothing. Which was annoying. But Nellie wasn't in a position to complain. Besides maybe he was tired of talking. He'd had to answer a lot of questions from the other ones. They must have asked every question under the sun. From favourite foods, to music, to whether people still wove their clothing, and all kinds of other stuff. Although Nellie couldn't complain about that. Even half-asleep she'd learned a lot.

The bus wound around the hill and Nellie could see the village behind them. Was she about to get raped? This thought was always on the edge of her mind. She looked at Marcos — they were about the same height but his arms were bulging with muscles and she was probably about fifty-five percent body fat thanks to three months of stuffing Reece's Pieces and potato chips into her mouth under Taz's disgusted gaze.

"You're never gonna get a guy eating like that," he said.

"Good," she replied, knowing that he was worried that she'd be living with him and Julie forever. As if Nellie would let that happen; she liked Julie but living with a couple was slowly killing her soul.

What if this driver raped and killed her? She would make the perfect victim — it's not like anyone was going to break the bank looking for her. Her mom would certainly try but the rest of her family weren't really the foundation-setting-up type. As for the Canadian government, she didn't think they were into hunting down international criminals who preyed on Native women when they didn't even do that in their own country. Nellie felt around for the beer bottle in her bag. That would have to do. Hit him a couple times, run down the hill, find a phone and call her mom. She exhaled; life was always easier when you had a plan, no matter how pathetic.

Marcos stopped the vehicle. Nellie craned her neck to see their destination. All she saw was a large white building stretching up.

"What's this? The church?"

"My house."

"Oh. Are you the mayor?"

Marcos laughed. "Come inside and meet my wife."

The front door was a light-coloured wood and Marcos knocked once before entering. A tiny woman wearing jeans and a T-shirt came around the corner and grinned at Marcos. "You're late!"

Nellie almost laughed. Marcos's wife was a babe. Even Julie would have a tough time measuring up to this goddess.

"This is my wife, Nina. And, this is Nellie, she only speaks English."

"Sorry."

Nina smiled. "Don't be. Most of the people around here speak different Indian languages anyway. English is a safe bet."

Marcos led the way to the dining table where there were large chunks of bread, dishes with chicken and fish; it was a veritable feast to Nellie's standards. There was wine too, which Nellie had tried once at a university party and spit up a second later. But she took the glass that was offered to her. With each sip, it got less disgusting. Nina was curious about her colouring and Nellie explained that she was Native Indian, Cree to be specific, and that she had grown up on a reserve. Marcos and Nina were interested in that; they plied her with lots of questions about Native people in Canada such as how were they treated and were they self-governing? Nellie answered them between sips of wine, wanting to make it sound better than it was but failing as the night went on.

She was pretty drunk by the time she found herself explaining that she was there because she had realized that the love of her life was a sex-crazed, drug-addicted drunk.

"How old are you?" Nina asked.

"Twenty-two."

"That's a good age to make new choices."

Marcos was bored with all the relationship-talk. "Just have fun, Nee-lee!" He topped up her wine until it nearly overflowed.

Nellie floated to her bedroom. She fell asleep thinking maybe she was the luckiest human being in the world.

Marcos and Nellie headed down to the worksite that morning. They brought coffee for the other workers. Everyone looked bright-eyed and bushytailed, except for Nellie whose lips were still stained with wine.

Noah sniffed the air around her and winked.

Nellie moved self-consciously away from him.

Marcos assigned them their tasks. The boys were to help with framing and the girls were being sent over to the community garden.

Nicole wrinkled her perfect brow, "I'm here to build."

Marcos looked at her arms: "Can you lift a beam?"

"I can do other things."

"You're a guest here — can you respect what I'm asking you to do?"

Nicole looked pissed. The two "M"s didn't look pleased either. Normally Nellie would have jumped on board with the ladies but she actually liked gardening and she certainly did not have the head this morning to listen to hammering and drills.

At the garden, a smiling grandmotherly type offered them aprons and gardening implements. Nellie went to the far end of the garden and stuck her earphones in. She had an entire Madonna compilation to keep her company.

She was on her sixth playing of "Ray of Light" when she noticed the sweat crawling down her face. She licked around her mouth and sucked part of her sweat back into her. She walked back to where the other girls were working.

"Water?" she said to one of the "M"s who nodded at a pitcher set on a table. Nellie poured a glass of water and drank slowly. Her stomach wasn't feeling too keen either.

"Where are you from?" Nicole was suddenly beside her, pouring a glass as well.

"I'm from the Saskatoon area."

"What's your family's background?"

Nellie immediately knew what she was getting at, "What are you?" Because this was a question people — white people — always asked her. She wasn't dark enough to fit their idea of what a Native was but her skin had enough colour that they knew she didn't belong to them. She decided to make her work for it.

"Farmers." Not exactly true — but her mom liked to garden, so . . .

"I mean, like where did you come from?"

"Canada."

"Originally?"

"Originally? Northern Canada. Like Bering Strait area."

Nicole's perfect brow was again disturbed.

Nellie had grown bored of this game. "I'm Native."

"Oh." Nicole's gaze looked her up and down. "I've never met a Native person before."

"Yeah, it's super-hard to meet a Native person in Canada where nearly a million Aboriginal people live." Nellie was already missing her solitude.

A group of young kids ran by screaming as a belligerent goat chased after them. Nellie half-smiled. She remembered goats from her uncle's farm.

"What kind of Native are you?" This from one of the "M"s.

"Cree."

"What was the reserve like? Was there a lot of poverty?"

Nellie had no idea how to answer that one. "Compared to what?"

"I'm from Edmonton," this from Nicole, "and one time I drove past Hobbema where they have all that oil money and I couldn't believe how many of the houses were boarded up or had graffiti all over them — why would people do that? Like just destroy things?"

Nellie's heart was pounding like that time she had taken on a professor who had said reserves were the cause of all Native social problems — the same place where tiger lilies grew and native kids swam in dug outs — that was the root of their problems? Nellie had wanted to punch him in the 'nads. But these were girls so instead she relied on an icy response: "How the fuck would I know?"

Nobody asked her anymore questions.

Nellie poured herself another glass of water with shaking hands and drank it down. Without making eye contact, she reached into her pocket and turned on her CD player again. She trudged through the dirt making a little dirt cloud behind her.

✦✦✦

Their workday ended at a little after two. Marcos came by with some food and water bottles for them. He announced that they were free to go do whatever.

"Like what?" asked Nicole.

"Anything you want," Marcos said. "The kids play soccer in the courtyard, you might like that. You can explore the village. Don't go hiking just yet. It's a bit dangerous in the woods — vipers, spiders and Zapatistas," he laughed loudly.

Noah laughed as well; everyone else seemed confused.

The only thing Nellie wanted to do was go back to her room in the beautiful white house at the top of the hill but she didn't think that would be fair to Marcos and Nina.

She hung around at the garden site and chewed on a carrot. Noah was gathering up people for a hike up to the old church at the other end of town. "It was built by the Spanish," he explained to everyone as if that was some kind of special enticement.

Nellie could feel the cold twinges of loneliness moving in so she nodded at him when he asked her if she "was in." Everyone else joined in unfortunately but that made sense. They were all strangers in a strange land (even though Nellie actually looked like she was from the area).

The girls were apparently still smarting from her grouchy rebuke and stayed away from her. And the two frat boys were obviously jonesing for a screw and so stayed close to the blondes.

"So how are you liking it?" Noah asked.

"You people ask a lot of questions," Nellie said and then regretted it. She couldn't alienate everyone. Could she? No she probably could.

"Prickly."

"No one wants to talk to me — just ask me questions."

"That is talking."

Nellie sighed sharply. "I guess I'm wrong then. I guess it's not that I'm being treated like a science project because I'm not white."

Noah was silent for a few steps. "Do you like socc- I mean, I like soccer. I like it a lot."

Nellie hid a smile behind her hand.

"I like soccer as well," she said finally. "Are you into all this Christian stuff too?"

"I am a youth pastor — for the United Church. So, yeah, you could definitely say I'm into this Christian stuff." He was smiling as he said this so Nellie was able to squelch her urge to smack herself in the face.

"Just don't try to convert me. The Mormons have tried, the Catholics, one time a Wiccan girl. I'm not a joiner."

"I converted like eighteen people last month. So don't worry, we don't need you."

They didn't have much time to continue their conversation as kids kept running towards them, firebombing them with questions. "Canadian?" "Polar bear?" "Buffalo?" These were the ones Nellie heard the most.

They reached the church. It was impressive compared to the other buildings. It was three stories high and the belfry had a giant bell in it.

"That is what woke me up this morning," Noah said.

"I didn't hear it."

"Seriously? That thing is loud."

Nellie pointed at the hill on the other side of the village. "I'm staying with Marcos and his wife."

"Ah, favouritism."

"First for me." Except if you counted lonely librarians and ancient elementary school teachers easily bought off with handmade cards.

One of the frat boys pushed open the church doors and they walked inside. Nellie looked around before entering — trying to make eye contact with the Mexican people watching them — was this okay? Nobody seemed concerned.

The church was what you would expect — pews, altar, artwork depicting the suffering of Jesus. Nellie gravitated towards a giant painting of Mary and an altar filled with flowers and tiny frames with pictures of loved ones. Nellie looked through the pictures, saw some pretty hot guys and wondered how many women in the village were experiencing the same heartbreak as her, how many had cried themselves to sleep too many nights to count, how many slept with their arms wrapped around a pillow missing the feel of him.

"Boo!"

Nellie jumped. "Fuck!" The word reverberated through the church. Nellie could see the "M"s shaking their heads in disgust though they refused to turn around.

Noah laughed. "You really are the worst, aren't you? Oh wait — you don't like questions. You are the worst."

"It's your fault. You scared me." Nellie smacked his arm.

"I did." He was unrepentant. "We're heading out to the graveyard, because this place isn't morbid enough. These are all dead people, I assume." Noah picked up a picture of a smiling toddler.

"Maybe. Maybe just people who are sick." Nellie took the picture from him and put it back on the ledge.

"We can hope. You coming?"

Nellie could feel fatigue spidering through her body. "I'll stay here."

"I'll come back for you."

Nellie shrugged. She stared at the big Mary painting. Mary looked beautiful as usual. Two thousand years and the woman hadn't had a single bad hair day. There were lambs at her feet and she had the baby Jesus on her lap. He was smiling up at her. Mary and Jesus were a little browner than usual and Nellie liked that.

Nellie yawned and sat down in a pew. She slowly slunk lower and lower onto the wooden bench until she was lying down. She put her dirty forearm under her head and prayed for sleep.

ððð

When she woke up, the church was cool and the lighting was moody. Mary looked slightly menacing as she gazed down at Nellie who was wiping drool from her arm and her cheek. She sat up in the pew and felt her bones crack from the wood — how could anyone get used to being homeless? She made the sign of the cross to the Mary picture, warding off that kind of unfortunate life.

Nellie walked outside and saw the others sitting on the steps. She felt embarrassed; they had waited for her.

"Would you like some water?" Noah held up a water bottle. Nellie nodded and took a sip.

They walked slowly back to the worksite because they were starting to feel aches and pains from their work.

"Good idea with that nap," Margot said to Nellie.

"I don't think I had a choice. I was sleep-napped."

"Better than being kidnapped." Noah joked.

"Hey what are those Zapatistas that Marcos was talking about?" Nicole asked.

Good question, Nellie thought.

"They were fighting the government, they opposed expansion, capitalism, NAFTA."

"Were they violent?" Nellie's stomach felt this was the most important question.

Noah nodded. "It got really bad a few years ago."

"A few years ago?" That wasn't nearly long enough to make Nellie's bowels stop twisting.

"It's calmed down a lot." Also, not helpful.

"So we're basically in Zapatista territory — which is a group of terrorists?" Nicole's tone was intimidating. Nellie could imagine she was a real terror herself if you got her angry.

"Terrorism really depends on which side you're on." It was obvious which side Noah and his dreadlocks were on.

Nellie looked around them at the townspeople who didn't stare at them, just threw them the odd curious look. She wondered which of them had fought the government. How many of these people were braver than she'd ever been? Probably all of them. Even that old man standing in that doorway picking his nose.

Nellie wondered if the people saw them as enemies because they were from a capitalist society or if they forgave them because they were students? And also, would the Zapatistas treat her differently because she was Native and not white? Times like these, Nellie wished for the stereotypical long black hair and high cheekbones of her brethren. Julie would be a Zapatista cover girl for sure. And thinking of her Nellie felt that lonesome feeling hit her so hard she sighed. Noah looked at her and she pushed back the feeling — she was here, not there. And besides, here was wine.

There was a social in the town square that night. Musicians broke out guitars and dancing started. Nellie tried to stick with clapping her hands and tapping her feet but nobody would allow that. She was dragged up a few times to dance with different men. Mexican men are bossy, she thought. It was a nice change.

The party broke up way after midnight and everyone headed back to their respective homes.

"I'd offer to walk you home to your palace but you've already got a ride," Noah said.

"Plus you have to walk Nicole home. Don't want her to get kidnapped by the Zapatistas."

"They have better things to do than kidnap hosers. Besides, she's covered." Noah inclined his head; Nicole was in deep conversation with a young guy with skin like Cadbury milk chocolate. *Nice pull.* Nellie had to give her points for great taste.

Nellie and Noah's gaze turned back to each other and they went silent. They each had a hand on their hip in the manner of people who want to look casual.

"Nellie!" Marcos called from across the courtyard.

"That's my ride." Nellie walked away without saying goodbye.

That night Nellie didn't fall asleep right away. She sat on the edge of her bed and looked out the window. This place reminded her of the reserve with the stars so big and bright, you felt like you could reach out and touch them. The air even smelled like the rez, fresh with a hint of cooking smoke. It had been three years since she'd gone home; how had that happened? *Because it's always supposed to be there waiting for my city-spoiled ass to return home,* Nellie mused.

Over the week, Nellie grew brown like a real Cree. She had forgotten to pack sunscreen and was too proud to borrow any.

She resigned herself to early wrinkles and embraced the sun. The brown made her eyes look different.

"Beautiful," Nina said to her over morning coffee. "Such beautiful brown eyes." And Nellie ducked her head and tried to think of a joke to fill the space.

The garden was growing fast and the girls were bored of gardening. Nellie and the others wandered over and watched the men work on the school. The framing was done and the guys mostly worked on the roof. "Look at them sweat their asses off." Nellie laughed, grateful that she got to keep her feet on the ground.

The other women couldn't leave it at that. They complained to Noah and the other guys over coffee. "These guys are sexists," Margot said.

"Not true," Noah replied. "Latin American feminism just isn't the kind you're used to."

"Easy for you to say," Nellie said.

Noah poured more coffee. Nellie couldn't figure out how he drank that stuff in the heat. "It was only a few years ago that women and men fought along side each other for the Zapatistas."

Nellie thought about how women and men had stood along side each other at Oka against the Canadian soldiers. She'd wanted to go there and join them. She'd even saved up a few hundred dollars for the trip. It had been the first time in her life that she had put something else ahead of school. But she ended up lending (well, giving) the money to Everett to fix his truck after his motor blew.

One day Marcos said that he was taking them on a trip that afternoon.

"Where?" Nellie asked. "I don't like surprises." They made her nervous.

"Then it's definitely a surprise." Marcos liked bugging her.

"There's a waterfall nearby," Noah's voice tickled her ear. She pushed him away.

"So this waterfall — can we swim in it?"

Noah grinned, "I will."

He did look like the kind of person who swam wherever he liked, with dolphins, stingrays, sharks, all those things that could kill you but looked fun. He probably surfed too. Did they surf in Vancouver? Lately, she had all kinds of questions about that place that she'd never given two shits about before.

They piled into their trusty van, though this time Nina joined them. She saw Nellie sitting at the back and gave her a questioning look and then took her place at the front closest to Marcos. After a few minutes riding alone at the back, Nellie moved closer to everyone else. She had been planning to take a nap.

The road was dusty and windy. Nellie was glad she brought her water bottle along.

Noah dropped next to her. "Isn't this exciting?"

"I've taken a bus before."

"This is the area that the Zapatistas held. It's where shit happened." Noah had never swore before. His hands drummed on the back of the seat.

Nellie glanced at Marcos' dark head. "You're wrong. He wouldn't put us in danger."

"They're not the enemy. They're like the Mohawks at Oka."

Nina had told Nellie that her and Marcos had been teachers a few years before. When the school had been burned down in the fighting, they had promised to rebuild. And applied to the charity that had sent money for materials. Nellie surmised that in exchange, the village had to take in a bunch of dumbass university students.

The van was slowing down. Nellie could feel the mood in the bus change as the brakes squeaked to a stop. She looked out the window and saw the green of a jeep and then she saw the black of guns. The last time she'd seen a gun, it was a .22 that her uncle had tried to hock to her dad for bingo money. This was no .22.

"Fuck." The youth pastor was really on a roll today.

Nellie could see two hands reach across the aisle and clasp together. Nellie thought that was a bit much. She called out in a loud whisper to Nina but she didn't turn around — her posture was straight as an arrow.

Nellie looked at Noah who was biting his lip and drumming his hands again. She stilled his hands with her own. "Why do they have guns?"

"We're Canadians," Noah said after a long pause. "We'll be okay."

"Ha." Nellie wasn't sure that was the cross to ward off all attacks that he thought. "What do they want?"

"They're looking for Zapatistas." He whispered the last word.

"But they're all — " Noah put his hand on hers and squeezed it. She dutifully swallowed the rest of her sentence. Then he nodded at Nina.

Where did the Mohawks go when the fighting was done? Home. To fight a different way.

One of the frat boys moved closer to the front of the bus to get a better look. "Sit down," Nina hissed at him.

Marcos had gotten off the bus. He faced the soldiers, his hands at waist height, open and facing front. A soldier was talking to him. Marcos answered. Then he turned back to the bus and gave them a half-smile.

He can take care of this. He knows what he's doing. Sit still and we'll be on our way. Things will take care of themselves.

Yeah, right.

She remembered once driving with her mom past a couple walking down the road, the woman slightly ahead, the man a few steps behind. Nellie was only ten and telling her mom a story when her mom slammed on the brakes, threw off her seatbelt and ran out, the car still running. Nellie watched in the rear-view mirror as her mom launched herself at the man and pried his hands off the woman. Then she held herself between them, like a denim-clad X.

The soldier went back to the jeep to talk to the other soldiers. Nellie thought *this is taking too long.*

She was moving now, between the rows, she knocked the hands apart.

She heard Nina's urgent, "Nellie," but she kept going. The gravel was under her feet and she moved quickly but not fast enough to startle anyone.

She stopped with a metre of Marcos with her hands on her hips: "Mark? What the fuck?" Marcos looked at her, his look unreadable. But probably mad.

But Nellie could be bossy too. "I paid to see the waterfall, not to sit in a shitty bus roasting my ass off." Nellie had only used her valley girl voice to make fun of white girls and she knew she sounded phoney as hell. But what the hell, right? Valley girls seemed to lead perfect, safe lives . . . Nellie needed some of that glossy luck right now.

The soldiers were looking her up and down. If only she wasn't so brown — *why didn't I wear some fucking sunscreen?* — but she didn't know what else to do, so she continued, "Who's in charge here?" Although she had no idea what she would say to anyone who declared themselves in charge, probably just crap herself. One of the soldiers bit out, "*Sube al autobus.*"

Nellie rolled her eyes. "What? I don't speak Spanish."

Marcos looked like he wanted to push her into the ditch. There was a shadow beside her — it was Noah. "Dude, we paid good money to come down here — your boss is going to hear about this."

"Like seriously," Nellie added. Her eyes met Marcos. He seemed resigned: *Okay you stupid kids, you win.*

Marcos put a look on his face like he'd been harassed by tourists for too long. He held up his hand to Nellie. "It's okay, Miss. It's okay."

Nellie turned back to Noah and tugged on his arm. "I want to go back to the resort," she whined. But she really wanted to go home to put her head on her mom's chest and hide there for a hundred years. She looked at the bus and saw the others standing then, their white faces so blinding that you didn't notice Nina.

The soldiers went back to the jeep, the guns slung over their shoulders at least. Marcos looked at Nellie and Noah and his look said it wasn't over yet. And it wasn't. The van was searched — for drugs, they were told — and money was paid, not a lot, a few twenties among them all. And then the bus was turning around. Even as they drove away, Nellie felt like they could not go fast enough.

That night they had dinner at Marcos' house. Her hand traced the mouth of her wine glass as everyone crowded together around their small table. Nellie felt her denim shorts pressing against Nicole's linen pants and Noah's hairy calf brushing against her hairless one.

"You're a hero," Noah nudged her.

"I should have my status card taken way for that little performance."

Noah laughed. "Oh the irony."

The frat boys were re-telling the story with embellishments about pissed pants and dirty shorts.

She thought about the dinners she'd had with the couple. *Have fun, Nellie. Smile Nellie. Enjoy yourself.* The kind of advice her mom gave her whenever they were close; her mom who only ever wanted her to be happy.

But others wanted more. Her dad told her she had to go to law school because "our people need fighters." The chief of her reserve had given her an eagle feather after she graduated, "You make us proud," which could have been a congratulations but felt like an order. (Taz had told her law school would take away what little Indian she had in her to begin with.)

Instead of being a warrior, I'm pretending to be a white girl in a country of brown people.

Her world was safe and easy because other people had fought the battles and wore the scars. Nellie closed her eyes and saw the faces of those people she grew up with who never made it anywhere, whose faces she had only in her photo album and that one face that still woke her at night.

Nellie felt herself falling then.

She reached for her wine glass with a shaking hand, felt her mouth begin to tremble and wondered how she could get away from all of them without embarrassing herself. *This is too much.* And then his face flashed in front of her. His easy smile, that made you smile too, no matter what stupid things tumbled out of that mouth. Hundreds of miles away and she could still hear his voice: "Nellie, chill the fuck out." Calm settled into her bones. *I hate him*, she reminded herself but there was no conviction.

Around the table, glasses were raised and Nellie offered hers.

Princess

August 1997

Without asking anyone, Nellie signed them all up on a slo-pitch team. She said she told them but Everett couldn't remember her mentioning it. Still he called up Taz and Julie and convinced them to go because it was something different. Julie booked off that weekend and Taz cleared his schedule of eating shit and playing video games — dude was getting fat and he wasn't even twenty-five. He didn't want to do it, he was bitching up a storm to Everett the day before saying Everett should control his old lady.

Everett shut him up by telling him he needed the exercise. He could tell that Taz wanted to say something to him but there was nothing he could say. Everett had spent the whole summer working a road construction job and his gut was as tight as a drum.

Normally Everett didn't like to spend the whole summer working but this job was different. The contractor running it was this character who strolled through life high. They took ninety-minute lunch breaks to smoke weed and play poker. Even the flag girls were fun, hot and flirty as hell. At the pace the job was going, it was going to take another year to finish the tiny bit of highway they were working on and that was fine with Everett.

Everett thought it was kind of hilarious how Nellie kept bragging to all her friends about his new job. If only she knew how little he was working. But that's how she was, as long as he left in the morning and brought a paycheck home, she was happy. She was predictable and he wondered how she got like that. It didn't seem very Native to him to do stuff in the same way all the time.

He had tried to explain this to her a few times but she told him that was lazy-person thinking and to stop being such an idiot. And to grow up. People were always telling him that too, like as if they all knew what being grown up meant. He sure as hell didn't. Sometimes during a break at the job, he'd hear some guy talk about how much trouble he was having maintaining his lawn or not having enough time to work on his golf game or how he didn't know how to handle his kids and Everett's eyes would glaze over. *People really wanted those problems?* Seemed like a whole different world.

The ball field was a long ways out of town, out on Beardy's Reserve. Everett wasn't a fan of playing on teams he didn't know; he had to trust that Nellie had signed up enough people. Turned out that all people she'd signed up — mostly, law students — never showed up so it was left to him and Taz to find the rest of the players.

Everett played first base, Taz was the catcher and Julie stood way off in the field. Everett told Nellie to play the field too but she was determined, "if I'm gonna play, then I'm gonna play," and was clinging to third base with a determination that was kind of admirable even if she was useless and missed the ball as often as she caught it.

They lost their first game and clawed their way to a minor victory in the second. Nellie had spent the entire last inning cheering from third base because the guys had stopped throwing to her. Everett wished she would shut up already. She ran up to him as he walked to the dugout and put her arm around his waist so that they had to do that awkward huggy walk.

He slapped hands with the rest of the players. He'd brought in a few of his construction friends and Taz had asked some guys from his work to play as well. They were a good group, someone had thoughtfully remembered to bring beer and he cracked one and turned to watch as Julie walked all the way in from the outfield.

"Fucking hot out there," she said, her face had a mist of sweat on it. Her skin had already turned brown after one day in the sun like a real Indian. It made her teeth shinier and her hair blacker. Well, not all the way black, he saw shades of red in it.

He handed her his beer wordlessly. She took a long sip and thanked him with a smile. Taz curled his arm around her and ruined the moment. He whispered something in her ear that made her laugh.

They decided to go to KFC for lunch. The team arranged itself in booths. Nellie sat next to Julie, Everett and Taz sat across from them. Everett kept leaning over Taz to talk to Jamie and Eddie, two guys from Everett's site who had all kinds of funny stories. Jamie was in the middle of one about some woman he'd met over one of those phone dating lines and when he showed up at her house, it turned out she was in a wheelchair.

"Thought something was up when I saw the ramp, the door opened and I thought well what the hell, a pussy's a pussy, right?"

Everett felt rather than saw Nellie stiffen up but ignored it. He should have known that wouldn't work.

"A disabled person is still a person," she said loudly.

"Nobody's judging, he still fucked her," Taz replied.

Everett chuckled.

"Don't laugh." Nellie's eyes narrowed like a snake.

Don't be this way, Everett would say under his breath if she was next to him. But she was too far away from him so he gave her a look instead.

"And, don't look at me like that. It's not right to laugh at disabled people. Any one of us could become disabled and then would you think it was so funny?"

"If I was disabled," Everett said solemnly, "I'd be honoured if Jamie wanted to bone me."

"And I would!" Jamie yelled from his table.

Julie giggled so the guys started to pile on with their jokes. Everett could see that Nellie was fighting her natural instinct to create a scene. She must have been tired from scrambling around under the hot sun because she switched her focus to her chicken and fries and kept her opinions to herself.

"How are you all friends?" asked Jamie. "You from the same reserve?"

"We three grew up on Stone Man's," Julie pointed at Everett and Nellie and herself.

"It's called Asinîy Napew First Nation now," Nellie butted in.

Julie pointed with her lips at Taz. "And this one is from way up north. That's why he's got those Dene eyes."

"And that backwards sounding Cree accent," Nellie added.

Everett could never figure out why Nellie needed to poke that sleeping dog.

"Yup, I'm a real Indian. Not a fake-ass, mostly monias Indian, like these ones. Crow's Nest First Nation." Taz proclaimed.

"Pelican Lake," Jamie said and he and Taz punched fists.

"That's cool, you guys stayed friends your whole lives," Jamie added, "that's how it is on my rez too."

Nellie nodded, "Yup we've been friends since we were kids."

Everett wondered if you could be friends with someone you never talked to. He remembered seeing Nellie at the front of the class in elementary school, a chubby kid with a squeaky voice, hand always in the air, ready to answer every question or add something to what the teacher said. He didn't pay attention too much, there was always some action going at the back of the class. And, by the time he got to junior high, he was already in those slow learner classes. Of course he knew Julie, his cousins used to tease him about her. He remembered how she was so small for so long, nobody ever would have thought that she'd sprout such long legs.

"We called Jules here, the Shrimp," he said, smiling at the memory of the tiny girl with the big smile.

"I don't remember that," Nellie interjected.

"Ha! As if! My friends and I used to call Everett Shy-baby," Julie grinned back. "'Cause he would write me love notes and leave them in my pocket. Then when I tried to talk to him, he would run away."

"That wasn't me." Everett could feel his face getting red.

"And even if I wasn't in your class, you would always give me a valentine. They were real cute homemade ones."

Everett remembered going to his uncle and asking him how to spell the words, "Julie" and "forever." But he could never tell them that. "Ch, as if. I don't remember that."

"Yeah, you're right, I'm probably mistaken, must have been a different Everett Kaiswatim." Julie winked at him.

"I remember my schoolyard boyfriend," Nellie said.

"Who, the janitor?" Taz joked.

Nellie's mouth tightened as everyone laughed and Everett felt bad for her. He still laughed though.

Outside in the parking lot, they waited near the car as Taz smoked and talked to his friends. Everett knew the guys but didn't feel like talking to them. All they ever did was shit talk the chiefs down at the Assembly — sounded like jealousy to him. And when they weren't talking about that they were talking about the shit they were buying. Fuckers seem to have money to burn for doing nothing in Everett's opinion. If he took all the shifts he was offered at work, if he stepped to being foreman like his boss wanted him to, he could be making big money too — and his money would be clean — none of this government money. But he didn't see the point. He made enough money to get by, what else did he need?

Their last game was a tough one. The other team was so strong even their girls could play well. One of them, a real solid built chick, she even hit a home run.

In the dugout, Nellie said, "Someday I'll do that."

Everett wanted to explain to her that girls like that played all the time, that you couldn't just get that good at twenty-five but Nellie would call him negative and unsupportive so he didn't say anything.

The next inning, Everett hit a two-run homer and caught them up. Then Taz surprised everyone by hitting another one directly after. Everett watched Julie hug him as he headed back to the bench.

"Next game's at 8:00 AM," Everett told the team as they were packing up and everyone groaned.

"I'll bring coffee! Just show up!" Nellie pleaded. "If we don't have enough players, we forfeit — which is the same as losing!"

They know that Nellie.

They were the last to leave because they had to make sure all the equipment Nellie rented was there. Then they piled into her car. On the way home, Taz said there was a cabaret on that night.

"I don't know," Nellie said, "I have a paper to write and we have the game tomorrow."

"We're gonna head over, I hear the band is good," Julie said. "Plus Taz's friends will be there."

Count me out then, Everett thought. He remembered a huge spliff he had in his other jacket pocket and thought about how much fun he'd have smoking it on the deck of his house.

"I can buy your tickets," Taz said.

Everett hated the way Taz always assumed he was broke. "I have money. I just don't wanna go."

"Okay, fine, who gives a fuck."

It was a long drive home so Nellie suggested a game. Everett figured that it was something she made up because it didn't make any sense to him. Nellie asked all these "what if" questions and they answered them. "What if . . . you had all the money in the world?" Questions that eight year olds would ask each other. He didn't mind playing along because Taz pulled out a blunt he'd scored off his friends and passed it around.

"What if . . . you could change places with anyone in the world — who would it be?"

Everett knew this one right away. "That Hugh guy, the one that owns all those strippers."

"Hugh Hefner, owner of Playboy," Taz corrected him.

"Yeah, that guy. He's got the fucking life."

"That's charming," Nellie said, "Enjoy your gonorrhoea."

"I would test the girls first," Everett said knowing that he wouldn't.

"Anyone else?"

"I don't want to be anyone else," Taz said. Everett looked at him in the rear-view mirror, his arm around Julie's shoulder. God, he was such an asshole.

"That's a good answer," Nellie said. "I wish I could say that. But I would want to be Whitney Houston because she's the best singer in the world and she's got her head on straight. And, she and Bobby Brown make such a cute couple."

Everett wondered for a second if Nellie was secretly into black guys.

"Are you into black guys?" He asked.

She laughed so hard she spit all over the steering wheel. "Threatened, are we?"

She had gone down to Mexico. Maybe she'd been hooking up with black guys down there. Were there even black people in Mexico? He'd always meant to check where Mexico was on the map but never got around to it.

"Julie, you haven't said. Who would you be?" Nellie asked when she straightened herself up.

Julie said a name but it got lost in the breeze flowing through the car.

"What's that?" Nellie yelled.

"She said Princess Di." Taz said. There was never any chance of that guy not being heard.

Everett looked back at Julie and smiled. He could see her as a Princess, wearing fancy things and dancing in big rooms. He could see her visiting sick kids and doing all that charity work that rich people did because they had too much time on their hands.

"Why her?" Nellie yelled back.

Julie leaned forward between the seats. "She's got nice clothes and she gets to travel all over the world. And her kids. She's got two cute little boys."

Taz laughed. "She's Princess Di and you're Princess High." Julie elbowed him and Everett could see that her feelings were hurt.

That guy had a way of ruining every moment.

Nellie dropped off Taz and Julie at their place and then parked in front of Everett's house. Everett got out and heard her car door open after he opened his. *I guess she's staying.*

They had sex. Afterwards Everett pretended to fall asleep so that she would leave. She kissed his forehead as she left. He heard her moving through the house, muttering about research papers and what was the point when no one read them except for bored grad students.

Once she was gone, he headed to the kitchen. He turned on the radio and raided the fridge. He was frying up a bacon and egg sandwich when he heard the news come on. It was announced twice: Princess Di was dead. Car accident.

He left the sandwich in the kitchen and headed out to his back patio. He could feel people being sad. He lit up his joint and took a couple long drags. He thought a prayer in his head that he heard his mom say once, "May your spirit find its way home." And that was that.

About half an hour later, Taz walked in with a twenty-four of beer jangling under his arm. Everett glanced up and could see bruises forming on Taz's face.

"I got jumped."

"I can see that."

Julie walked in and shut the door behind her. She looked tired.

"Who was it?" Everett asked.

"Some guys. Being all territorial and shit. Would've helped if you'd been there."

Everett could smell a lie. "What did you do?"

"You got ice?" Taz headed for the kitchen.

Everett looked at Julie, she had curled herself up on the couch.

"What's it about?" he asked in a low voice.

"Taz was telling people that one of the chief candidates raped a girl and his cousins heard about it."

"Was it true?"

Julie shrugged and picked at a piece of lint on her T-shirt.

"Politics, fucking awesome." Everett got up and turned off the TV. He turned on his cassette player perched just above and turned on some music, old school AC/DC, all the way from the 70s. Music that was a little bit older than him.

Taz came back into the room with a pack of hotdogs held to his face. "You should've been there," he said over the music.

"Every man's gotta get a lickin' now and then. Keeps him honest," Everett laughed, and took the remainder of his joint out of his pocket and sat back down.

"Have a beer," Taz said.

"Nah, not feeling it."

"Suit yourself, I'm gonna get shitfaced."

Everett looked at Julie. "Did you hear?"

She nodded.

"Fucking crazy man," Taz said. "We were just talking about her today."

The phone rang in the other room but Everett was too lazy to get up. He could feel a pain in his calves that told him maybe he was getting old after all.

Taz laid down, with his head on Julie's lap. She petted him like a dog.

Everett thoughts went back to that pretty lady and how he'd been seeing pictures of her since he was kid, he thought about her kids and how they wouldn't have a mom now and he felt bad for them. Then he said under the cover of the music, "Nobody ever gets what they want," and pushed them out of his head.

Two Years Less a Day

January 2000

THE ROOM WAS LARGE which Julie liked. Everything else she hated. The blinds on the tiny windows were dirty and hanging off sideways. The desk was littered with paper. Small yellow Post-its, white forms, notebooks, and file folders were scattered everywhere. Everything had a fur of dust covering it. A sticky determined dust that would gather on your fingers if you dared to disturb it. She felt like attacking the room with a mop and a couple gallons of javex.

Julie heard a plop. It came from the big, fat, wine-coloured jacket hanging on the coat rack that was still wet from the snow and radiating cold. There was a brown puddle around the base. Julie imagined someone slipping in it and breaking their neck. She noticed her thoughts taking these dark turns these days but didn't have the energy to rein them in.

Across from her was a woman, a short-ass, which was what Julie called anyone who was round and short. The woman had dyed her hair a beige blonde, "the colour of baked bannock," is how Julie would have described it to Nellie. The ends of her hair were still damp from the snow outside.

When she'd walked in, the woman had been at her desk, turning on her computer with one hand, taking her jacket off with the other — she looked frazzled as shit which didn't give Julie much confidence.

The way you do one thing is the way you do everything. Julie had heard that somewhere, probably from Nellie.

"Julie Papaquash?"

"Yes, I came to talk."

The woman held up her hand. "First, I need to read your file."

"But — "

"Please sit down."

Julie felt like standing but she'd already learned that requests were demands and demands were orders and any disobeying made the guards come running.

Julie was thirsty. The building was dusty wherever she went and no matter how much water she drank, it was never enough. Before she went to bed, she filled a cup from the sink next to the bunk bed and drank from it over and over again while her roommate, Shells, watched, got bored and turned over.

"So where do we start Julie?" The woman looked her over and Julie felt her unwashed, greasy hair sticking to her head, felt that pimple that was beginning inside her nose and red heat climbing from her chest up her neck to her cheeks. In the real world, this conversation would be like trying to ask a friend to lend you money after you'd run over their dog.

"I need to get out of here." Ten days ago she had walked into this shithole and her heart immediately started beating faster. That feeling was only getting worse. Every morning she woke up feeling like she would start screaming and not stop. She stayed away from windows because she wanted to smash them with her fist and force her way through. She didn't tell this woman that though, that would be a one-way road to seg.

"I don't work on that sort of thing. That's a legal matter." The words slid out of the woman's mouth, the way people said, "Fries with that."

Julie felt the wind knocked out of her like that time she'd slipped on the ice in front of her building. She was in the air long enough to know that when she came back to earth, it was gonna hurt like a bitch. She was right.

The woman went on, "As a caseworker, my job is about making your stay productive. I'm about making use of your time. None of us have very much of it you know. Goes by in a flash." She attempted to snap her fingers, but they were soft and pudgy and only made a soft "swoosh" sound.

Time does fly — unless you spent the night before staring at a crack in the ceiling next to a picture of a penis exploding — then the seconds seem to be stretching on like years. Julie swallowed her anger along with the bile she felt rising up her throat.

She took a deep breath and exhaled noisily. Nellie blew up all the time at salespeople, waitresses, Everett, but they were small fires, easily contained. Everett just got mad, punched people and then was done — his anger dumped out like garbage. With Taz, anger was as natural as breathing. You could see it in his posture, corded through his muscles. But Julie never got mad, never raised her voice, never raised a hand to anyone.

"I hope you don't mind me saying, but you're very pretty."

Julie stared at her. *Am I allowed to mind anything?*

"I'm sure you hear that a lot." The woman put her pen in her mouth and slipped it in and out a few times, making it sopping wet with her spit. "What program would you like to take? We have openings in GED."

"I have my grade twelve."

"Are you sure?"

"Grainfield High 1992."

Julie even had a school jacket until one of her aunts stole it.

"Okay, well, we also have a carpentry course. No, wait, that's full up. Oh here we go, I have an opening in substance abuse in three weeks."

"I'm not much of a drinker and I don't do drugs."

"You sure?" The woman's voice had a smile in it.

Julie took a deep breath and nodded. This bitch was getting on her last nerve.

"It says here that you were drinking when the fight occurred."

"That was a lie. I was at home, I was watching TV. I was alone." On my own for the first time in my life and this shit happens. Why don't you move in with me, Nellie had asked her and Julie had laughed, "we're too old to be roommates." Because she couldn't say that she wanted to be alone for once, wanted her own little place to decorate how she wanted, her own kitchen table to sit at and think.

"I'm going by the court record." The woman tapped the document in front of her, like it was a Bible.

"It's not true."

"But that's all I have. You see when you're convicted — that means the court decided that this is the way it happened. And

I know you think the other person lied but the judge believed them and not you. It may not be fair but that's how it is."

"I want to appeal — how do I do that?"

"You can talk about that with one of the guards — they have paperwork — "

"But the guard says she ran out — "

"Then you wait." The woman's voice was sharp. "In the meantime . . . " The woman poked the edge of Julie's file with a surprisingly beefy index finger. "You need to get in line for programming."

Julie looked at the ceiling and caught her tears.

The woman looked back down at Julie's folder. "You were in foster care for a while."

"Yeah."

"Ran away a few times."

"I had some aunties who lived in the city. Sometimes they'd let me stay with them."

"Is that when you started turning tricks?"

"What?" Julie sat forward.

"Says here you were 'flirty with men and known to hang out in pick-up areas'."

"Who wrote that?"

"Mrs. Wallace."

"Who?"

"She was your social worker when you were thirteen."

"I met that woman like once."

"I guess you made an impression."

"When I was thirteen, I was still playing with dolls." *Stolen dolls from Kmart, yeah, but dolls.* "Why would you even have that file? I wasn't charged with anything. I didn't have a record. And I thought juvey files were sealed anyway?"

"Are you done interrupting me?"

Julie blinked.

"I'm going by what's in the file. This is what I was sent. This is what I'm working with. Now you can get up and leave right now. But I'll have to put it in your file that you didn't want to cooperate." She smiled. "Or, you can calm down."

"It's a fucking lie."

The woman reached for the phone, "Are you gonna be calm?"

Her hand hovered above the phone.

"I'm calm."

Julie sat up straight, she smoothed her pants with her hands before raising her eyes. "I'm not a hooker."

"It doesn't matter to me. I'm not here to judge, I'm here to help you get better."

In her mind, Julie was dragging this bitch around the room banging her face into the radiator and the heavy metal desk.

"Julie?"

Julie stared at the fat wine jacket and watched the water slide down the seams. There was a dark red patch where the water had collected.

"I'm calm." Julie could barely hear her own voice. *Who is that answering for me?*

"That's better."

"Write it down. Write it in the file."

"All right. Inmate states that she is not a prostitute." She wrote slowly with a smile on her face.

Julie looked at a point between the woman's eyes. She and Nellie had taken a yoga class together once and she remembered how the instructor kept talking about that third eye. Julie focussed on the woman's as her favourite rhyme bounced through her mind: "I am rubber you are glue, whatever you say bounces off me and sticks to you." Then her mind leapt to an image of herself sticking a chopstick through that third eye.

"Now which program do you want me to put you down for?"

"Carpentry."

"It's full. Do you have a second choice?"

Julie's stomach rumbled. "Substance abuse."

"Are you sure? You say you don't have any addictions. How will this help you?"

Julie knew the kitchen was closing in ten minutes and she knew that it would be well past noon before she'd get anything to eat again. She gritted her teeth. "I think everyone can learn something from substance abuse training. Like how to control your emotions."

The woman's puffy cheeks swelled into a grin. "True."

"Can I go now?"

The woman gestured towards the door.

Julie stood at the door. The woman reached under her desk and a buzzer sounded. Before she stepped through, Julie looked back. "What's your name anyways?"

"Marguerite." Her voice had a sing-song quality.

∽৯∽৯∽৯

When Julie was a kid, she spent her time outdoors. Mostly that was in the city. But she spent time in a foster home that was on a farm. The family had a tree house that the dad had built for his daughters. They hated it, preferring to play video games inside, so Julie took it over. She spent one afternoon tying a rope to the branch next to it so she didn't have to clamber down the tree all the time, she could just go down the rope, burning her hands every time she did. When the girls saw that she'd changed their tree house, they told her that she had to take it down or else they would tell. Instead of taking it down, she pulled the rope up and stayed there the rest of the day.

Around suppertime, their dad walked over to the tree house.He checked the knot and told Julie to be careful.But she didn't need to be; outside was always safer than inside.

When she thought about it, she couldn't remember a single day when she didn't go outside at least once in her life. Now there were several strung together.

The doors buzzed open at 7:30 AM and Julie dragged herself off the top bunk. Shelley or Shells as she liked to be called, had been there first.

"Besides," Shells joked, "you're so goddamned tall, you could just step up there." They lined up at the front of the cell. Sometimes leaning, sometimes standing straight. Shells said morning to the women on her left and the women on her right. She made jokes about wet dreams and waking up with her pillow between her legs. She teased others about moaning in their sleep. She told them that Julie was a champion farter: "Nearly tore a hole through the mattress — better check your panties later!" No mistake about it, Shells was a morning person.

After they were counted, the ladies marched towards the cafeteria where they picked up their trays and lined up again for breakfast. After that everyone headed off to their jobs, Julie and Shells working in the laundry, which was hot and damp. So you had to watch out — once you got damp, if you got hit by a draft, you were shivering for the rest of the day. It would have been unbearable if it wasn't for Shells who joked all the time and made the hours pass quickly.

"So what did the white lady tell you, Bambi?" Shells asked. She coined the nickname because she said that Julie's eyelashes reminded her of a baby deer.

"No programs for what I got."

"What's your problem?"

"I don't have any problems."

Shells laughed. "That's worst motherfucking problem you can have in this joint. Now get your bony ass over here and help me load these sheets. Can't believe this is an institution for women with all these goddamned shit stains!"

Julie spent her evening in the TV room, sitting in the second row of couches, nearest to the phones. She leafed through a decades old version of *Chatelaine*. She liked knowing how people were decorating their houses back then. They probably thought they had them all done to perfection and then now they were finding out that their style looked like shit.

She kept her eye on the phones. They were allowed one call per day but with four phones and a hundred women, they were always tied up. Shells said it was because once the women got on the phone with their kids, they wouldn't get off. "Fucking sad bitches mope around for the rest of the night too," Shells added. It was the first time Julie was grateful that she didn't have any kids.

Julie heard Shells' big laugh and turned to see what she was laughing at. Shells was playing cards with a bunch of other women. They were all older women (compared to the other inmates). Mostly in their thirties and forties, they were Native with a couple of dirty blonde white women mixed into the bunch. This was Shells' court and she presided over it with her loud voice and dirty jokes.

"Bambi! Come play this hand for me?"

Julie looked around the table. The ladies didn't look scary.

"Don't let them cheat you," Shells handed her cards to Julie. "I'll start you out with three smokes."

Julie balanced them in her hand.

"Good night you pack of dumb bitches."

Then to a chorus of women telling her to go fuck herself, Shells sauntered out of the room.

"She's got a date," a woman with one side of her head shaved said as she dealt out the cards.

"Did that start up again?" Another commented.

"Never learns."

"Girl's got needs."

Julie studied her cards trying to figure out what game they were playing.

"So what are you in for?" The blonde lady — Julie thought her name might be Carrie — asked.

"Assault."

"I thought you were a working girl."

Julie wanted to get mad but felt this wasn't the right time surrounded by a bunch of women she didn't know.

"Just a waitress."

"Too bad, you could make some decent coin."

"Sometimes I make them buy me a beer first."

The women laughed.

There was a banging on the door behind her to the lady's lavatory. Two young girls, with fresh skin and dark eye makeup, were leaning against the door and laughing.

Shaved head tsked. "Little shits."

The banging continued and the girls kept laughing.

"They got their friend locked in there," Carrie said. "They won't listen to me. Someone yell at them."

One of the women at the table obliged. The girls gave her the finger.

"Ain't listening to nobody."

The banging continued and the women ignored it. Julie won a hand of what she figured out was a type of poker. Her pile grew to ten. Shells would be happy.

Two guards, a man and a woman, showed up at the door. "What's going on?" the woman demanded.

The women looked in the direction of the bathroom. The guards marched over.

Julie didn't get to make her phone call that night.

≈≈≈

Three days later, Julie was back in Marguerite's office. "I can't call out," Julie said.

Marguerite shook her head ruefully. "That's what happens when people don't follow rules."

"But I didn't do anything."

"But you were there."

"What was I supposed to do?"

"You were supposed to report them."

Nobody told me that. Julie could say that but then Marguerite would reply that ignorance of the law is blah blah blah.

"Can I use your phone?"

"My phone is not for inmate use. There is a phone in the rec area and just outside the kitchen."

"But they're both locked down. I told you that."

"There's also the phone outside the guard's office on the second floor — "

"It's not a real phone, it's restricted — "

"You can call your lawyer or you can call the ombudsman and report a complaint. Any time of the day while you are out of your cell."

"I don't have a lawyer. That's why I'm in here. When can I use the phone?"

"You say you saw the girls?"

"Yeah, like every other person in the room."

Marguerite pulled a paper from her drawer. "You wanna sign something saying that?"

"Can I use a phone then?"

"I always help people who are trying to help themselves."

Julie signed the paper. Marguerite handed her the phone. Julie felt her fingers shaking as she dialled. The phone was busy.

"I gotta dial again."

"Sorry kiddo, I got another appointment coming in."

"But I didn't get to make my call!"

"The Director says that she'll let people start making phone calls as of Monday. As long as you all behave yourselves."

Julie's head pounded.

❦ ❦ ❦

Julie folded sheets. She tried to beat her number from the day before. She hated it when they made her switch from sheets to clothes because then her count was wrong.

Shells poked her in the side. Julie looked at her impatiently. Shells was leaning on the shoulder of a large Black woman. Nobody touched people as much as Shells did, probably because they'd get a fist in the face. But for some reason when Shells did it, it was okay.

"This is Adrienne."

"Yeah," Julie didn't stop folding.

"Adrienne says there's a class tonight. Creative writing."

Adrienne nodded.

"I'm not a writer," Julie said.

"It's taught by this stone cold hottie. Fucking line-up to get into this bitch a mile long. Fucking idiots here sign up just so they have something to bone themselves to." Shells paused, "But I see you doing some writing in this class."

"I'm not a writer."

Shells looked at Adrienne, "I told you she ain't too bright. God rarely gives brains and beauty — except in rare cases." Shells slapped her hand on the sheet, stopping Julie's motion. "It's a writing class with a civilian. Who comes here and then leaves here. Get it? Adrienne, here, handles the sign up sheet."

"Five," Adrienne said.

Shells poked Julie in the ribs, "Pay the woman you heathen."

Julie's hands shook as she counted out the smokes and handed them to Adrienne.

∽੭∽੭∽੭

The creative writing class was taught by Mrs. Dixon who was pushing seventy. She stood so straight she looked like she ironed her bras. She read them some poems by a woman named Emily Dickinson — "she kept to herself most of her life," Mrs. Dixon explained and Julie envied that — what she would give to have a room to herself for ten minutes. After her readings, Mrs. Dixon gave them some time to write a poem.

Julie had written a poem once, about a bird she saw that was eaten by a cat. One of the lines had been "its guts sprayed out all over the sidewalk." This time, she spent the writing period drawing a picture of a cat.

The ladies read their poetry at the end of the class while Mrs. Dixon stood at the front of the class with her arms folded and her eyes closed. Some of the women really got into it. One woman even cried as she read her poem about how much she missed her kids. Julie got kind of misty too so she made herself focus on the mole between Mrs. Dixon's eyes that looked like a knot of wood.

At the end of the class, Mrs. Dixon told them she wouldn't be back for a few weeks. Julie looked for the guard but she was talking to an inmate.She moved fast but not too fast that she would scare the old lady.

"Hey."

"Yes?"

"Just this." Julie handed her a piece of paper folded up seven times.

"What is it?"

"I can't call out of here and my friend is the only person who can help me get out."

"Do you know how much trouble I could get into?"

The guard popped her head in. "What's going on?"

"Just asking her about poetry." Julie tried to sound casual even though she could feel a vein poking out on her forehead.

The guard raised her eyebrows. "Let's go Papaquash."

Julie walked out without looking back.

∾ঙ∾ঙ∾ঙ

Julie was cut from her laundry job. The guards said that they were all talking too much so everyone got reassigned. Julie was one of the newcomers so there was no place for her to go. She sat in her cell with a book on her lap wishing that she liked reading.

She prayed. She remembered that one time she saw this documentary on an Indian family — not Canadian or American — East Indians — and they were praying. They really got into it. They kneeled and bowed and sang. Maybe that's why her prayers never came true, she never threw herself into it. She got her knees and clasped her hands in front of her. The hard cement was punishing on her bony knees. She whispered into her hands, "please, please, please . . . "

She would have continued that way indefinitely but she heard the heavy step of a guard and quickly got up and sat down on the bed. People would think she was some crazy religious chick.

As the guards footsteps got nearer to her, Julie held her book closer to her face. So she was surprised when the guard stopped at her door. "You have a visitor."

ᪧᪧᪧ

Nellie was sitting at a table when Julie saw her.

One time when Julie was little and her mom and her got separated in a store, she actually ran into her mom's arms when she saw her and her mom had said, "Ch, as if."

Julie never did that again.

Julie crossed the floor and sat down at the table. She looked at the guard station, the cameras, the other tables . . . She didn't know what to do with her hands. When her eyes found Nellie's face, she saw that it was pink with fury. She almost smiled.

"They took my fucking phone!" Nellie hissed. "Checked my ID twice. Fucking gave me a pat down. My boss told me to wear a suit so that wouldn't happen and it still happened. I feel like I'm visiting Pablo Escobar — what are you in for anyways?"

"Assault."

"Taz?"

"My neighbour."

Nellie growled. "That bitch. I knew she was gonna be a problem with all her fake sweetness, 'if you need anything, just let me know.'"

"I guess they decided to believe her instead of the person who can't fake sweetness . . . "

"You're naturally sweet — anyone could see that."

Julie remembered the judge's cold eyes and how he interrupted her every time she spoke until her answers were curt and defensive and she knew she could feel the ground crumbling beneath her when she opened her mouth, how she'd tried to smile and knew from his eyes that she looked cocky, not honest. "How's Everett?"

"If you can believe this, he's in jail too."

Julie's smile was faint.

"My boyfriend is in jail and my best friend. I have got some fucking issues."

Julie nodded, wanting to say something funny, but the tears were already leaving her eyes.

Nellie rubbed Julie's hand. "You can't fucking cry. If you cry, then I'll cry and then we'll look like a couple of lesbian lovers sitting here comforting each other."

"You're too short for me," Julie sniffled.

"I may not be hot but I am a lawyer. Well, almost."

"Got Kleenex?"

"No. Sorry. They kept my purse on the other side."

Julie wiped her eyes and nose with her sleeve. "I need to get out of here."

"Who was your lawyer?"

"I didn't have one."

"Why didn't you call me?"

Julie had thought about this every single night since she'd been locked up. "Because I didn't do anything."

Nellie grimaced. "Okay well just tell me everything."

Julie told her in one long sentence. Nellie had that intent look on her face; Julie called it terrier-face.

ﷻﷻﷻ

Julie sat in the second row of the TV watching area. She wasn't
paying attention to whatever problem the sitcom family were
solving with gentle good humour. She felt her blood singing
and a secret smile forming beneath her skin. Shells plopped
herself down on the edge of Julie's chair and half on her lap.
Julie would never get used to Shells' casual affection.

"I need you to stay here for half an hour."

Julie glanced at the clock. "I can stay for an hour, if you
want."

"He doesn't need an hour. He's fucking limp dick pig with
shit for brains. But goddamn his hands . . . "

"Clock's ticking." Julie did not want details.

Shells practically skipped out of the room.

❧ ❧ ❧

Julie watched two episodes of *Home Improvement* before she
meandered back to her cell. She'd never watched so much
damned TV in her life.

When Julie got to her cell, Shells was sitting on her bunk,
her eyes on the floor.

"What's wrong?"

Shells didn't look up.

Julie had learned a long time ago that if people didn't want
to talk then you shouldn't make them. She reached for Shells
blanket and pulled it around her shoulders.

Then she climbed on her bunk. A few minutes later lights
went out but Julie didn't hear anything from the figure under
her bunk. No sniffles, no tears. She stared up at the exploding
penis.

The next morning, Shells was in her bed, the covers pulled over her head. She stayed that way even as the cell doors opened, even as the female guard came in to check on her.

"What's up Shelley? You feeling okay?"

Shells made no answer. Julie risked a look back. The guard was pulling back Shells blanket.

"Looks like you got a bit cut up here, hey?" The guard's voice was soft. The woman next to Julie slapped her arm hard and Julie risked another look.

"Her arms are cut up." Julie whispered to the woman.

"How bad?"

Julie shrugged.

The guard came through the door and yelled at the guard in the office. "Get a nurse on D-block, cell 48." The women started to chatter.

The guard turned to Julie, "You see her do this?"

Julie shook her head. "Is she gonna be okay?"

The guard ignored this and shooed them down the range. "All right ladies, let's go. Breakfast won't wait."

❧❧❧

Julie had spent the morning cleaning the cell. The guards had done a piss poor job and when Julie requested some rags and cleaning supplies they let her do it. She'd always loved cleaning to be honest, liked seeing the difference that hard scrubbing made. She washed the floor until she could see the lights glinting off it.

She picked up her pail and waved at the guard as she headed to the bathroom. She dumped out the pail and felt relief as the pinky water went down the drain. She rinsed it a few times and then began to wash her hands. They were red and peeling in places. Julie needed a lot of moisturizer to fix them — but when would she get that? "It'll grow back," she reminded herself.

She heard the bathroom door open with a bang. Three girls came in. Their intent was so obvious that it would have been funny except that she never could laugh when she felt like puking. What made it worse was that Julie knew this was fun to them. *What kind of things did people do to them,* she wondered to herself. Nellie would say it was no time to get philosophical . . .

They made a semi-circle around her, slowly forcing her into a corner. They were laughing but Julie could see it was forced now. She wanted to tell them this was too much. That she was already having the worst day, her friend was sick and she didn't even know how bad. But Julie knew they already knew that, or else they wouldn't be here.

Julie had aunties who were tough ladies. One of them broke her husband's leg and the other nearly paralyzed some woman outside a bar in Ft. St. John. They'd been telling their fighting stories to her since she was a kid. She knew how the story was going to play out.

Except for the stabbing, that was a surprise.

⋘⋘⋘

Julie only heard the next part, the guards over her, arguing whether or not it was serious enough for the hospital or if the nurse could handle it, because she kept her eyes tightly closed like she was on a roller coaster. She knew better than to put her two cents in; plus she was concentrating on stopping the flow of blood from her abdomen. *Stop, stop, stop,* she repeated inside her head, followed by, *clot, clot, clot.*

She could feel the wet spot spreading across her tummy even underneath the strong hands of the paramedic applying pressure. *He knows what he's doing* she told herself, her lips making the words but not the sound. Finally someone said that they would get into big trouble if the inmate got infected. *I'm Julie.*

The ambulance drivers loaded her up with no muss or fuss. She heard the handcuff click as they loaded her onto the gurney. She flicked her eyes open when they hit the open air so that she could see the sky as they rolled her out of the building.

Three days at the hospital and then they shipped her back to the infirmary. The infirmary had a nice bed. Julie noticed that right away. She never made a big deal about beds when she was dating Taz and he used to take her to nice hotels but after a month on a metal bunk bed, she sure noticed the difference. Her back felt like it was being hugged. *I'm getting old.*

Nellie came to visit her and did this whole *Terms of Endearment* routine where she bitched at the nurses until one of them sniffled and those were some tough ladies. (Julie had just asked for some ice chips.)

Julie asked Nellie to look for Shells among the beds. And Nellie did, sticking her head around privacy curtains even. But Julie already knew she wasn't there. Shells would have been by her bed by now, telling her which nurse was a closet druggie and which doctor had a big dick. She would have told Julie what she thought of Nellie: "Seems stuck up," And Julie would have said she's not, you only have to get to know her.

Julie was still in the infirmary when she met her lawyer, the first she'd ever met other than Nellie but she never thought of Nellie as a lawyer. Kevin was a small-eyed white guy with narrow lips and a huge nose, the biggest she'd ever seen. She liked it on him. He filled up the room with rants about the institutional racism of the justice system and the racial profiling of First Nations people. He pounded his fist on the table and said that she would not be another victim of a system that allowed tragedies like the starlight tours. He was so offended, he made Julie smile, though she tried to hide it. She didn't want to hurt his feelings.

Nellie's visits were a lot longer than visiting hours allowed because Nellie said the words "civil suit."

"So you sleeping with my lawyer?" Julie asked one evening.

"Are you fucking crazy? He's my boss."

"But I don't know when I can pay you back."

"Please as if I would make you do that. I never made you pay me for that pair of shoes you ruined on New Year's Eve."

"The heel was already half off when I put them on."

"Liar." Nellie pushed the ice chips at Julie. She believed they held magical healing powers.

"I'm not the one paying," Nellie paused for effect. "Taz was concerned."

Julie's stupid heart leapt. "How is he?"

"He's his same ole shitty self. He asked me if my acne was from eating bad food or from an unplanned pregnancy — is that even a thing? God he's annoying." She scratched her chin absently. "Please do not fall back in love with him."

"Okay."

"Besides Kevin would do this for free if you went on a date with him."

"I'm not a hooker."

"Gees Louise, learn to take a joke."

～ら～ら～ら

Everett got back the day before Julie did. He was in the car with Nellie when she walked out with her garbage bag filled with her stuff. He jumped into the backseat to make room for her. He leaned between the seats and teased her:

"Heard you did some hard time?"

"Idiot, she was stabbed."

"How's that going?"

"It's gross but it's alright." Julie figured it was going to scar and it shouldn't bother her because she wasn't the type to wear bikinis, but still . . . it sucked. Who wanted reminders? "Where's Taz?"

"In jail," Nellie said dryly.

"For real?"

"No, he's in Ottawa. Had a job interview."

Julie felt sad at that. She'd been looking forward to strong arms.

That night they drank at Nellie's. Julie noticed some new furniture; no more cardboard boxes used as coffee tables. Nellie started crying twice for God knows what reason. She'd be drinking and talking and then her head would fall on the table and her shoulders would heave. Julie sipped her beer slowly, wanting the night to last.Everett finally took Nellie to bed after she started crying for the third time.

"You're home," she hiccupped and she touched Julie's cheek before Everett ushered her away.

Julie turned up the TV to give them privacy and to interrupt her thoughts. It didn't work. She thought about Shells, she thought about the women's faces in the bathroom, she thought about always being wrong no matter what she said. She felt a breathless feeling like her heart was going burst out of her chest. She wanted to go to the bedroom and ask Nellie and Everett to help her but she didn't think her legs would hold her.

She didn't even feel like she could scream. Her heart was racing like a maniac and Julie thought: *this is it.* This was how she was going to die — from a heart attack, one day out of jail with a beer in her hand. She closed her eyes and tried to remember the third eye but all she could see was Marguerite's smirk.

Everett tapped her on the forehead. "Jules."

She opened her eyes. He was grinning at her.

"Your beer is empty."

He bit the cap off a beer, handed it to her and then pushed her over on the couch with his butt. "Y'know, the first time I went to jail, I was twenty. Everyone said it was gonna be like a party and I'd see my cousins and we'd hang out and play cards and work sometimes and order McDonald's and it wouldn't be shit. And it wasn't a big deal." He took a sip. "Except for some parts."

Julie took a long sip. Then wiped her mouth with the back of her hand. It was still shaking.

When she could trust her voice, she asked: "Were you able to forget it?"

He nodded, without smiling. Julie noticed for the first time that his face wasn't handsome without the trademark Everett Kaiswatim grin.

Julie pulled at a thread that was coming out of her jean jacket. "Do you know how my mom died?"

"Nellie told me someone killed her."

Julie flinched at that. She didn't like the "k" word. "Yeah. She went with this guy and he said she tried to rip him off and he beat her up. Then he dumped her in the woods."

She looked at Everett. He didn't look all shocked so she went on: "The cops had to cut a deal with him so that he would tell them where she was."

"Fucker."

"They still didn't find her until the snow melted." The jacket thread was short and she couldn't pull it all the way out. She gave up and smoothed it back down with her fingers.

"Nobody deserves that."

"I remember thinking that if a person's mom died, you would know in your heart. But I didn't. I had no idea she was gone until they told me."

Everett took the remote and turned up the TV. Then he kissed her.

The Great Mystery

June 2001

THEY DROVE OUT OF the city in Everett's old truck, scratched and dented, bald tires and zero shocks, but still chugging along. They were on the road for about an hour before they passed a dirt road and Everett skidded to a stop.

He laughed, "Fucking almost missed it."

Taz searched the side of the road and saw a sign sticking out the side of the ditch that said, "Kaiswatim," and an arrow pointing to the west.

They bounced down the dirt road kicking up soft black dirt behind them. Taz glanced in the rear mirror and thought about how far away their dust cloud could be seen. Weren't these ceremonies supposed to be secret or something?

"Going to a wedding with Nellie next weekend. Gonna get wasted."

"White or Indian?" Only white people had open bars.

"Indian. Two weddings this summer already . . . fuck me, man, she always gives me this look." Everett showed Taz what Nellie's glare looked like.

Taz saw where this was going and he had no sympathy for Everett. "You've been together almost ten years man. Shit or get off the pot."

"What about you?"

"She wears my ring. I asked her years ago."

"That's not the same thing."

"No but we're waiting until . . . " Taz paused. He couldn't remember what he was actually waiting for. But then Julie never pushed for stuff like that, probably didn't even care about it actually. When he gave her the engagement ring, she made a face and said, "Do I have to wear it?" And he was like, "Of course you have to fucking wear it." Sometimes she was so weird.

"Until you hit the jackpot?" Everett joked. "Thought you were making a million bucks working down at the ole Chiefs of Saskatchewan. All 'dem fancy suits and shoes."

Taz shook his head. Could this fucking idiot be any more stupid? "It's office attire."

"Fancy fancy."

"Nellie is being called to the bar this year, isn't she?"

"Yeah. And her family will be coming up and it'll be all the questions and I don't even think her family likes me — "

"What's there to like?"

"Fuck you. Anyway . . . I've got a plan."

"Borrow enough gas for the Mexican border?"

Everett laughed. "Nah, fuck that. I'm gonna do it. I'm gonna go for it." He pointed at the glove-box.

Taz opened the dusty box and reached around until his hand closed around a tiny velvet box. One of those. He flicked it open with his fingers; it was an ugly damn ring. Gold, which

Nellie would hate. A big pink stone in the middle, which she would really hate. And some rhinestones all around it. Something a dumb reserve Indian would think was fancy but looked cheap to everyone else. "She'll love it," Taz said.

"I guess. Nellie's not picky."

Taz had to look out the window to hide his smile.

He had some of his own news to tell but they were pulling up at the camp. Or at least it looked like a camp. There were two more trucks, about as beat up as Everett's parked next to one another. Then miles of waving grass, high as a man's thighs. There was one tree off to the right with fabric blowing in the breeze. In front of them was a brown structure with rounded edges, like a beaver's dam. Taz had seen a few lodges on his reserve when he was younger though his family didn't do that kind of thing. They were United Church all the way; the minister used to eat Sunday supper at their house.

As he opened the truck door, the smell of burning sweet grass greeted him.

⋖⋖⋖

Everett met Lincoln at a powwow. He'd been hanging around with some drummers, which led to meeting some pretty little Fancydancers when this old man in a cowboy hat flagged him over to a picnic table. "You a Kaiswatim?" The old man asked when Everett ambled over.

Everett nodded and sat down.

"Who's your dad?"

"Oliver Kaiswatim. Don't know him though. My uncle raised me. He's a Pratt."

"Right. You know your other relatives on that side?"

Everett had never bothered looking for them. He figured if his dad couldn't make the effort, then why should he?

"Nah."

"Oliver's sisters were looking for his boy. You know Freda or Pauline?"

"Never heard of them." Everett turned his eyes towards the Fancydancers lining up for Grand Entry.

Everett gave one of them a grin and she blushed. He turned back to the old man who was giving him a measuring glance — like he didn't know if he liked him or not.

The old man pulled out a rollie. "You got a light?"

Everett pulled out a lighter with Michael Jackson doing his Thriller pose on it. He'd stolen it from a drug dealer.

"What's your name?"

"Lincoln Kaiswatim. I'm your Mushum."

✥✥✥

Taz was surprised how firm the old guy's handshake was. "Call me Linc," he said with that accent that said that Cree was his first language.

"This your first time?"

Taz nodded.

The old man explained the protocols and the general process. He said if it got too hot, they could take a break. Other than that he told them to be quiet and listen.

Taz and Everett stripped down to their shorts. They hung their towels on a tree outside. Everett crawled into the lodge first. Taz followed at a safe distance. It was dark in the room but he could see faces in there: mostly old guys, a couple guys a bit older than him and Everett and a teenage boy.

It was hot.

Definitely hotter than the guys at work had explained. Some of them went to sweats practically every weekend and so were probably used to it. Although Taz couldn't figure out how you got used to this. He could feel his face turning red, then a shade of purple. Sweat was already dripping off his chin before an old guy started to sing.

He was the first to take a break. He crawled into the still-bright sun and it felt cool though it had to be at least thirty degrees. He was dizzy, hungry and weak. He wanted to walk to the truck and fall asleep in the box. But he had to go back in. Everett was still in there. The old guys. That fucking kid.

He wished for water. He pulled up some of the cool grass beside him and chewed on it.

ᗧ᙮ᗧ᙮ᗧ᙮

It bothered Everett that he didn't know what the songs meant. It bothered him that Taz knew and he didn't know. Why hadn't anyone taught him Cree, anyway? It bothered him that he didn't feel anything. Wasn't he supposed to feel something? Other than feeling hot? He stared across the fire at an old man. His eyes were squeezed shut as he sang. Everett wanted to reach each across and hit him. *Stop singing, make this stop.*

But he knew enough about ceremony that it wouldn't stop until long after you wished it were done. He closed his eyes and tried to think of something cold. Ice. Snow. Scraping his windshield in the winter. Feeling the cold of the steering wheel sink into his wrists. He was doing well — he even felt that dull ache. Then he felt the warmth seep into it, filling it up again with this hell. How much water did he have in him?

He wished he hadn't gotten drunk the night before — wasn't booze dehydrating? He wished he hadn't had that coffee on the road. He wanted to run as far away from here as he could get but knew he didn't have enough liquid in him to get him to the doorway — why did he sit so damned far from the doorway anyways? Taz had sat close and it was an easy crawl for him out the door. Everett closed his eyes again. He tried snow again but saw only hair. Long hair. He opened his eyes and stared across at the old man. The old man's eyes were on him. Stern. Like he caught him siphoning gas from his car or something. Everett closed his eyes again. Hair again. Her face taking shape. He covered her with snow and it melted off. He stuck his teeth into his tongue. *Nope. I'm not going there. Not going there.* He opened his eyes, this time he stared down at his hands so that nobody's eyes could meet his. He saw ropes in his hand. *No.*

There was a swing. *Mary had a little lamb, my little lamb, his fleece was white as snow.*

Shhhhh . . . he said. *Stop singing.*

His fleece was white as snow and everywhere that mommy went, her lamb was sure to go.

He felt the tears on his face and shut his eyes tight.

∾ઉ∾ઉ∾ઉ

Back inside, Taz knew it was only a matter of time before he would have to go out again. He kept his breath shallow and listened to the songs. Better than doing nothing. The east, the west, the north, the south. Healing. Cleansing. Come inside.

It would be easier, a part of him drawled, *to let the wind inside if you left the lodge door open.*

He half-smiled. The effort making him sweat even more if that was possible.

Part of the deal was that you had to feel something. Something bigger than yourself. A chief told him that one day. You may not start out that way, but you will get there. And the most important thing — and he said this in a warning voice — was to keep returning to that connection.

Julie. Sometimes he could smell fresh hay in her hair and he wondered where that smell came from. How could you still smell fresh and innocent after twenty-five? He knew he smelled like the inside of a hockey bag at the end of the season. He smiled in the darkness.

And now there would be another Julie. A long-legged doe-eyed girl. Or, another him. That might be too much for his old heart.

He laughed. Sharp and loud. The old men responded by singing louder.

ৰ্দৰ্দৰ্দ

Afterwards they lit a fire and the old men told dirty jokes to one another. Taz laughed long and hard. He looked over at Everett expecting to see his dumbass laughing in that silent way he did. But he wasn't laughing. His face was pale.

Taz elbowed him. "What's up with you?"

"Hungry."

"There's soup."

"Yeah." Everett didn't seem interested.

Taz shrugged.

One of the old guys started coughing pretty bad. Taz glanced over, it was Linc. The cough had that full sound to it like he had a lungful of something. He coughed and coughed and coughed.

"Maybe you should get him away from the fire?" Taz suggested to the people watching this.

One of the old men shook his head.

Linc caught his breath. "It's from the lodge," he rasped. "Whatever sickness people are carrying, it gets shared."

Taz wondered about that because he'd never felt stronger.

"We going back?" Taz asked Everett — it was getting dark already. Everett looked at Linc and then shook his head. "Not yet."

"Shouldn't be in such a hurry," Linc said.

"Some of us got work tomorrow."

"Work," Linc spit on the ground, a long brown line.

Yeah, work that pays for people like you. But he couldn't say that. Not in a place like this. This old man was king here. Taz clenched a handful of weeds and grass in his hand. He'd felt so clean only a second before and now he felt as low as a piece of garbage. That's how these old guys were, always pissing on the younger generation, even though they drank like pigs and beat their wives when they were younger. And now they were all holier than thou.

"Hey," Everett's voice was craggy, like he had a cough in it too. "Shake it off."

"Fuck you." Taz said. He got up from the circle. Maybe he couldn't leave but he didn't have to stay there. These weren't his people, probably wasn't even the right ceremony for him.

ক্ষীক্ষীক্ষী

They slept in the back of the truck and just as the sun peeked over the horizon, Everett told Taz that he'd have to hitchhike back to Saskatoon.

"I'm headed to Crow Fair. My grandfather wants me with him."

It took a few seconds for this to sink in. "Are you fucking kidding me?"

"Yeah. I mean no, I'm not kidding. I have to go."

"You have to go right now?"

Everett nodded. His face was still. The guy was dumb as meatloaf but Taz knew once he made up his mind, the Hulk couldn't budge him.

"You can forget about the gas money I was gonna give you."

Everett nodded. "That's fair."

Half an hour later, Taz watched the truck drive down the road, two heads inside bobbing to the washboard roads. He swore at his friend and began the walk back to the city. He was a least a mile into his walk when he realized he'd forgotten to tell Everett about the baby.

911

October 2001

ALONE. MIDNIGHT. BAR.

Julie liked none of those words.

She stared at her phone and thought about the phone call she wasn't going to make unless stuff got out of control. She was in control right now.

I'm not cold. I'm not hungry. I'm empty.

Besides, Nellie would ask too many questions. She had already called the other one and his phone was cut off. And then there was Taz and she would never call him.

Three. How do you get to almost thirty and only have three people in the world?

I should trust more people. Put that on a tattoo. She already had a tattoo; it was a blue hummingbird on her right shoulder blade. Nellie told her they move their wings really fast. "You walk slow, you talk slow, you do everything slow. It doesn't suit you at all. Should have got a flower or something like that."

Julie got it because it was blue.

The bartender walked past and asked her if she needed anything, she smiled as she shook her head. She had fifteen minutes, tops, before she'd have to head back into the cold and trudge to the bus depot. Nellie once told her that her definition of poor was having to ride the bus. Julie would have to tell her that poor was riding the bus and not having enough money for a bag of chips.

Julie always hated purses. She felt weighed down by them. Now she had one more reason for hating them; purses can be easily stolen. Fortunately her ticket had been tucked into her bra, her phone in her pocket, her pills in the other.

Julie had a cousin on the north side of the city but didn't know her number. Maybe she didn't even live there anymore. But it was a destination. If she got there and her cousin wasn't home, then at least that would be three hours gone. Then four more and it would be daylight and her bus would be leaving again.

I'm not hungry. I'm not cold . . . Well, I'm a bit hungry.

She pressed the numbers on her phone even though the number was saved in her speed dial. Nellie's name popped up. She would be mad, she would judge, she would be bossy, she would be Nellie.

Most of all she would make Julie tell her everything.

When they were younger, Julie could keep her out — silence, a joke, an angry question thrown back in her face — but Nellie had learned her tricks. That was the trouble with people; they wouldn't leave stones unturned. They flipped them over and then poked at the nasty stuff crawling around underneath. But Nellie meant well. She just couldn't help herself.

"Stop drinking, break up with him and mean it, stop moving around, figure out what you want to do with your life." This lecture had started a few years ago when Nellie got herself together, as she put it. Julie missed the days when they were both broke and living in a basement suite with cardboard boxes as furniture.

Now Nellie was a "success" and didn't look at the price tags when she shopped. She had an assistant and she got impatient with service people. Her hours were scheduled from 6:00 AM to 9:00 PM but she always had time to give advice to Julie.

"I'll help you. Whatever you want to do with your life, no matter what it is, even a housekeeper. I will help you be the best housekeeper you can be. But if you are a housekeeper then at least try to start your own housekeeping business. I read that the woman who runs Molly Maid is a millionaire."

Julie wanted to crawl between some clean sheets and sleep a thousand years.

A man sat down next to her. Not exactly close but the bar was empty so Julie knew that meant something.

Men always sat next to her. Smiled at her with half-closed eyes. They pulled over when she was walking; they held doors for her. They stared through windows; they banged into doors. They followed her. They whispered. They catcalled. They whistled. They lied.

Julie wished she could make herself invisible. Then she could sit here or near the warm fireplace in the corner and sleep for a couple dozen hours. When she woke up, she would know what to do. She barely slept on the bus and she hadn't slept the day before then. She probably looked like day old shit.

"Buy you a drink?"

Julie hesitated. Her painkillers had that "no drink" sign next to them. But then again, she'd also been told to go home and take it easy. She nodded. The bartender was waved over. He poured the drink and Julie saw the hint of a knowing smile.

Fuck you, you don't know.

Two drinks later, her phone began to vibrate as the buyer-of-drinks was in the middle of a story about his trip to Panama. She could barely follow why he went doing there. *Fishing? That couldn't be right, who the fuck flew someplace just to fish?*

She looked down at the phone; Nellie's name was at the top of the screen. She used to have the name saved under Bossy but had changed it when Nellie saw it there the last time they visited.

Julie excused herself. Manners, that was a bad sign. It meant that she was trying. *And what are you trying to do Julie?* Her voice had a singsong rhythm in her head.

She walked across the bar to the far end near the fireplace. She looked through the wall of windows as she walked; it was raining now. Why did she always leave when the weather got shitty?

Because I have no choice.

"Hi."

There was nothing on the other end but sputtered moaning.

"What's wrong?"

"Everett." Nellie stumbled over the name, rolling her "r" and making his name sound kind of foreign.

"What'd he do?"

"Bwoke up with me." More tears, more sobbing. Then hiccupy crying. Julie stared at the flames turning red, then green, then yellow. Nellie was a few months older than Julie but she always seemed so much more hopeful about dumb stuff.

"You sure this time?" Their relationship was a broken vase that Nellie kept gluing together. And then once she got it to stand, she would proclaim, "Look at it! It's beautiful" while everyone else knew it was a fragile piece of shit.

Louder tears.

In her lifetime, Julie had only had one other crying phone call. Also Nellie. Also about Everett.

Her people never cried. Even when her grandma died, her aunt's phone call had been short but not sweet, "Kokum's gone. Come get your stuff."

Julie glanced over at the guy at the bar. He was talking to the bartender.

What do I do?

"What do I do?" Nellie's voice was still strong, meaning she hadn't been crying for long and the booze hadn't kicked in.

"Where are you?"

"At home."

"Go to sleep. You always feel better after a good sleep."

"I can't sleep. There's no way — I keep playing the conversation around in my head, *it's not working Nellie, it'll never work*. I slapped his face. I shouldn't have done that."

"Why not?"

"'Cause he'll think I'm mean and angry, one of those women who throws stuff. Guys hate that."

Julie shrugged even though she knew Nellie couldn't see her.

"Come over. I'll pay your cab."

Julie sighed — this was going to be hard. "I'm not in town."

Nellie's voice hardened. "Where are you?"

"Edmonton."

"What the fuck are you doing there?"

"Just visiting."

"When are you coming home?"

"A week." Julie could lie because Nellie couldn't see her face.

"A *week*? You're never here for me! I'm always there when you need me! You drive me crazy with all of your moving around! This is why!"

She was gone. Julie looked at her phone like they do in the movies. She was on her way back to the bar when it rang again. She sighed and answered it.

"Sorry."

"It's okay."

"Why did you leave? Did you have a fight with Taz? Did you break up?"

Julie used the lie she crafted on the bus ride up. "I came to visit some family. When did this all happen?"

"This afternoon. He took me on a drive with him to this old grain elevator. And he's all like, 'I want to show you something' and I thought he was going to, going to, going to . . . how could I be so stupid?" She broke off to wail again. Nellie hated it when she did something stupid.

"Yeah, I know. You guys have been together a long time. Anyone would think that." Except anyone who knew Everett.

"Why won't he love me?"

"He does love you but he's an idiot."

"But idiots get married all the time. Why can't I have my idiot?"

"If I knew, I would tell you."

"Men always love you. How do you do it?" This had a slight edge to it; Julie was used to that tone.

Julie looked over at the bar. The man was paying up. He looked over. She looked at the window, the rain was coming down in sheets. She looked at the bartender packing stuff up. Hotel bars always close early.

"Where are you?" Nellie's voice was small but still bossy.

"The bus station."

"What the fuck are you doing there? Where's Taz?"

"At home."

"Why didn't he drive you?"

"He was busy."

The man looked over.

"Look I gotta go. I'll call you tomorrow, okay?"

"Don't go — I don't want to be alone, I can't do this."

"I have to catch my bus."

"Bus? Where are you going?" Nellie's voice was razor sharp.

Careful, Julie. "I'm heading to Grande Prairie to visit my aunts."

"I thought you didn't get along with your aunts."

"No, well, sometimes. It's complicated."

"What's going on?"

Julie kept her tone light. "I felt like visiting family."

"You hate your family."

Julie laughed. "Not always."

"Well call me as soon as you get on."

"Okay I will."

Julie put the phone in her pocket. The man was in the lobby now. Sort of lingering and if she rushed . . . she'd look like she was rushing . . . but he'd probably like that.

Her pocket was vibrating insistently. Julie sighed.

"What?"

"I think he's already with someone else."

"That's how guys are."

"Omigod you don't even care!"

"Of course I care." *I'm going to sleep, sitting up in a fucking bus terminal for you.*

"Should I call him?"

"He broke up with you. He should call you."

"He's never going to call me. If we get back together it's going to be all on me. It's always on me . . . "

Julie walked through the bar. The bartender was turning off the lights.

"What am I going to do? I don't think I can do this again."

Julie looked through the hotel doors. Nobody on the streets. She liked that.

I'm cold. I'm hungry. I'm tired.

"Are you still there?"

"Still here." Julie opened the door, threw her hood up and walked into the rain.

The Aunts

THEY WERE IN THE front yard when she showed up. One was still in the driver's seat, the other was carrying in groceries, plastic bags making dents in her fingers. She walked up the incline and put her bag down before saying hi. One said hi, the other watched her from dark eyes and Julie knew that she hadn't been forgiven. Not after all these years. She walked in without invitation and sat on the couch that was hard and worn. They had a big screen TV. Even poor people found a way, it seemed. To the left of it was a fake fireplace. On the mantel was a meagre collection of photos. She recognized those eyes straight off and blinked.

They told her she had to buy her own food and pay them some rent, "We aren't here to help out freeloaders." They added. "You behave yourself."

The room wasn't a room; it was a pantry. There was a big bag of potatoes in the corner and neither of them offered to move them. She put down a sleeping bag and her backpack next to it. The room was so small that she couldn't sleep with her legs stretched out; she curled them up beneath her. Before she went to bed, she took three Advils and hoped this would be the last time.

When she woke up, one of them gave her the name of a construction company that was hiring. Julie poured herself a cup of coffee and drank it black. The construction company was nearly outside of town but a young guy saw her walking by the side of the road and gave her a ride. He was about seventeen with red hair. They didn't say anything to each other, other than, "Where to" and "Thanks." She'd never had that ability to strike up conversations and there was something about her that discouraged people from talking to her.

She found the foreman quickly enough. One of the crew pointed to a guy standing near a nice truck, "That's Nick."

Nick was a Native guy about thirty-five with thick unruly hair that was past due for a haircut. He didn't waste time. "Our flag-girl Chelsea left to go back to school. You ever done that?"

Julie shook her head.

He showed her a sign with "stop" written on one side and "slow" on the other. "I think you can figure it out," he said.

"I fucking hope so," Julie grinned.

He handed it to her and it swayed backwards in her hand. She straightened it. "After a while it gets heavy."

She got dropped off about half a kilometer from the worksite. There were big trucks coming in and out all day and at the end of it, Julie had a cough from the dust. It also got cold out there even though summer hadn't kicked it yet. She was shivering when Nick stopped by. "We're done for the day." Julie nodded and looked around her.

"You need a ride home?"

Julie jumped into the truck. She blew on her hands.

"It gets cold out there. Especially since you're just standing there. Chelsea used to wear a lot of layers."

"Okay."

He had a picture of two laughing kids on the dash.

"Cute boys."

When he smiled, his eyes crinkled at the sides and a dimple appeared. "They're wild as hell."

They rode in silence for a few blocks before he asked, "You got kids?"

"No."

She had him drop her off a few blocks from her aunts' place. Before she got out he said: "I can give you a ride home most days. But only after most of the guys have left, otherwise they'll talk."

Julie nodded, her eye on the gold band on his finger.

⊰⊰⊰

Julie told her aunts that she had a job. One of them asked for money but she explained that she wouldn't be paid for at least a week. She sat on the edge of the couch while they watched, "Wheel of Fortune." After they went to bed, she ate two slices of bread with nothing on it.

One time, she and Taz went to a fancy steak place. A second after their food arrived, they got into a fight because Taz said she was flirting with the waiter. The fight got so bad that they actually walked out without eating a bite of their food. Julie shook her head, they sure had been fools.

⊰⊰⊰

Julie doubled up on jeans and socks the next morning. She put two sweaters under her jean jacket. She caught the bus as close to the site as possible and then walked the last bit. When she picked up her sign, a few of the guys introduced themselves. They were grizzled veterans, their bodies slim and strong from a lifetime of lifting and carrying. They offered her some coffee and she gratefully accepted. She drank it quickly and then walked out to her road.

There was less traffic and the day passed slowly. Julie sang every country song she remembered under her breath and thought about what the writer must have been thinking of when they wrote it. She liked Dolly Parton who she thought was one of the smartest women ever born. Towards the end of the afternoon, the sun grew faint and it got cold. Julie did deep knee bends and squats and then finally push-ups to keep warm.

Nick picked her up around the same time. He told her about how one of the guys hurt his back because he tried to lift some wood by himself. "It causes a chain reaction," he told her. "I'll have two more hurt by the end of the week. Damn guys are superstitious as hell."

"I'll watch myself," Julie replied.

That night she went for a walk after her aunts had settled themselves down in front of the TV. "Don't talk to anyone," one of them said.

Julie closed the door behind her. She walked past a lot of homes like her aunts': televisions blaring, curtains closed.

There was a house with a group of young guys sitting on the steps. Two of them were holding skateboards, which seemed weird this far up north. They called out to her but she ignored them.

A few streets away, she found the library. She signed out a few books and then lingered near the magazines. She noticed a few native women walking towards a door and before she left she glanced inside. They were sitting around a large table, a collection of beads and cloth in the centre of it.

At work Julie had to work closer to the crew. A few of them walked out to where she stood to shoot the shit. Talk turned to the foreman. They were surprised at how well he was holding up. His wife was dying pretty fast from some kind of woman's cancer. "How long does she have?" Julie asked.

The general consensus was that she would be gone before Christmas. "Christ," one of them said and spit into the ground. "And him with two little kids. Can you imagine?"

Julie saw him across the field, deep in conversation with one of the sub-contractors. He said they always gave him trouble, always wanting more for a job than they asked for.

One of the crew lingered near her longer than the others. He was the youngest, just shy of thirty. He mentioned that there was a band playing at the bar. "Heard they were pretty good . . . " Julie declined gently.

ᕊᕊᕊ

On payday, Julie handed her aunts the money they'd asked for. Then she bought a warmer jacket, a pair of long-johns and some gloves. She also bought some groceries, which she put in a small corner of the fridge. She heard the aunts talking in the living room about how she'd be getting wild now because she had money. She didn't bother to tell them that she'd already spent all her money. Instead she crawled onto the mattress in her tiny room with a bag of chips and book and fell asleep before either was done.

ᕊᕊᕊ

She went back to the library on her day off. When she walked past the resource room, she saw that it was empty. She read the schedule on the wall: "Native Crafts Night" was every Thursday at eight. Kids were welcome.

Nick wasn't at work the next day. A few guys said that meant his wife probably died. But he was back next morning, sure of himself as always. At the end of the day, he told Julie that she should get herself a bus pass and she nodded.

"If you paid me more, I could buy a car," she said with a smile.

"I'm sure if you asked one of those old guys, they'd buy you one," he joked back.

"It wouldn't matter, I don't know how to drive."

He nodded. "I thought you seemed like that type."

"What type?"

"Kind of spoiled."

Julie laughed. "I wish."

"That's too bad," he said. "Every woman should be."

Julie had to breathe through a tightness in her chest.

That night she dreamed of Nellie. They were climbing some hill and Nellie kept telling her that something good was at the top. But every time Julie took a step, it crumbled beneath her.

Her aunts asked her where she was going one night. "To the library," she replied.

"Yeah, right."

Julie almost didn't go into the room. It was full when she got there and the talk was loud. It was probably the laughing that finally grabbed her.

The room went quiet when she opened the door. Then an older woman with long grey braids took control. "Hello, I'm Anita, you here for crafts?"

"Yeah."

Anita placed some hide, beads and a needle in front of her. She assumed that Julie didn't know what she was doing. She was right.

The conversation started to pick up after Julie got settled in. They were talking about some guy at the bar who always used the same line, "I hear Native women are the best kissers."

Apparently a couple of the women had fallen for it. But probably not anymore.

The mood was broken when a woman with thin hair that curled around her ears explained in halting words that her ex had refused to return the kids the week before. "He's all the way in Hobbema. He knows I don't have enough money to go get them." She was thinking of calling the cops but was afraid of social services stepping in. There was a lot of head nodding at this.

That had never been a worry of Julie's. Taz could be mean but he knew kids belonged with their mother. Whenever someone brought a baby around them, Taz would stare at the tiny round faces like they were aliens.

Julie stabbed the needle through the hide and found her finger on the other side. It hurt like hell but she didn't make a sound and nobody noticed.

Anita told the woman that she'd go down to the station with her. "Nothing else you can do. Otherwise you're stuck waiting for him to stop being a cocksucker."

The woman nodded but Julie could see she wasn't ready to get the police involved.

When it was time to go, Julie had beaded a small circle from some shiny yellow beads.

≼≼≼

The days turned cold. From morning to afternoon, Julie shivered, no matter how much she breathed into her hands or stamped her feet or did squats, she was cold. At night she coughed herself to sleep, the cold having found its way into her lungs. Around the site, guys were talking about their plans for the winter. One guy was heading up north to do some hunting, another guy was heading down to his place in Arizona. Julie could see what a luxury a good job was and wished she'd maybe thought about that sooner.

She was walking to the bus stop one night when Nick pulled up. She got in. Country music, Waylon Jennings, was blaring and he turned it down.

"Lucille," Julie said.

"Yeah."

"She was a real bitch."

Nick laughed. "I'm sure she had her reasons."

The lyrics danced through the vehicle, and Julie thought about that sad man asking his wife to come home.

"She probably went home," Julie said.

"She needed a break," he replied. "Kids are hard."

Julie looked out the window and saw her reflection nodding.

She reached for the heat at the same time as him and their hands met there. His hand strong and calloused on top of hers. Her breath got took. And then he pulled away.

"We're shutting down soon."

"I heard."

"I know the casino down the road is hiring. Dealers, waitresses, everything."

"Thanks."

Julie was distracted so she forgot to tell him to stop a few streets away. Instead he parked right in front and she could feel those eyes blazing through the drapes.

She left the truck with one last glance at those little boys.

By the time she got inside, the battle had already begun. They were both on their feet.

"That's a married man!"

"Knew she'd be at it in no time!"

"How long has this been going on?"

The larger aunt planted herself in front of Julie. She pushed her with big meaty arms and Julie swayed backwards. But she was pretty solid herself. She pushed back; her aunt surprised, stumbled and fell onto the couch. Julie kept walking.

"You get the fuck out!"

Julie packed her stuff quickly. It didn't fit in her backpack and so she had to walk into the kitchen to grab a garbage bag. They kept yelling but Julie had heard most of it before.

She came out of the pantry with both bags behind her.

"Once a slut, always a slut!" Her aunt pushed her again. Julie ignored it and kept walking.

The Aunts

When she was little, they told her that it was her fault that her mom went away. Because Julie was too hard to take care of and her mom got tired. Julie knew now that was grief talking.

She stopped in the living room and grabbed the picture off the mantle. They both attacked her then. But Julie wouldn't let go. She bit a hand that went in front of her face, she kicked at a leg with varicose veins sticking out of it and heard a sharp cry. The arms dropped away and Julie was suddenly out the door.

It was cold but her jacket was warm.

The Meeting is Cancelled

May 2004

IT CAME AS A text message as she sat at the airport. Her feet rested on her carry-on bag, her computer was on her lap. She was checking her online dating profile, "HotTamale11" when the message came through.

"Meeting is cancelled."

"I'm already at the airport" she texted back.

"Have a good trip?"

Lindsey, her assistant, was a twenty-seven-year-old redhead, married with three freckled children and had a laugh that made you want to be friends with her. If their roles were reversed, Lindsey would have laughed her way all the way to Toronto and dared the government to fire her when she got back.

As if. There was no way Nellie was going to Toronto by herself. If the message had come an hour later while she was on the plane then yes, she'd go set up meetings for herself and make herself busy. She'd head down to the hotel bar and have a drink every night and feel like a baller having twenty-dollar martinis until she picked up a dude. Usually only cost her about sixty.

But they sent the text in time and she stupidly replied to it. And now, they would cancel the trip, get the credit for the ticket (because they had a huge account and could pull shit like that). Reschedule the meeting and Nellie would go another time.

She got up, drained her coffee and hefted her computer bag over her shoulder. She pulled her suitcase behind her, admiring it as she did every time. It went forward, backwards, and spun in place. It could dance the merengue if she wanted it to.

"Nellie? Nellie!"

The voice came from the Chili's to her right.

She pulled her suitcase to the fence surrounding the Chili's as if their patrons needed protection from the hoi polloi. She glanced inside and saw annoyed people staring out at her. Then she saw him, his smile lighting up the darkness.

"Taz? What are you doing here?"

"Having breakfast. Where you coming from?"

"I had a meeting in Toronto."

"How'd it go?"

"It went fine." Nellie was too tired to explain everything and she was shouting over the heads of hungover-looking business people.

"Keep me company."

"I should get back to work."

"C'mon on, Loser. How often do we see each other? Like once every four years?"

Nellie flicked her wrist to the right and her suitcase obeyed.

She sat down across from him at a skinny booth. Why was everything in airports so small and cheap and plastic?

"Where you working these days?"

"Province. Ministry of Labour."

"What the fuck for? "

"I do good work."

"You do but the rest of them are a bunch of fucking assholes."

Nellie silently agreed. "Where are you working?"

"Indian Affairs."

"Oh for fuck's sakes, that's a thousand times worse."

"Land claims. I'm a hired gun. I come in and bury the Natives in paperwork."

"Gross."

"Pays well."

"Enjoy that blood money."

Taz lifted his drink and sucked it back. Nellie caught a whiff of it as he put it down.

"Jesus, Taz it's 10:00 AM."

"It's happy hour somewhere in the world. Let's fly there."

She had the air miles to do it. She had a suitcase full of freshly laundered, neatly folded business casual outfits. And one very sedate suit. And a little black dress that had never been worn, no matter how many times she packed it.

"I have to work tomorrow. And today, actually."

"Yeah, me too." He waved the waitress over.

The waitress was a slim blonde who made Nellie immediately regret everything she'd eaten in the last ten years.

Blondie smiled sweetly at Taz (*far sweeter than Taz deserved*, Nellie thought. But she'd always thought waitresses had a special kind of patience for bullshit).

"Deux. Of whatever this was."

She giggled, "Whiskey."

Nellie looked sideways at the interaction in front of her — was Taz really attractive to this young girl with every kind of option in the world? Nellie supposed his heavy-lidded eyes and big lips could appear sensual . . . if you were desperate enough.

"Those better both be for you. I don't drink that shit." Nellie said loudly.

"Oh right, you drink red wine 'cause you're so fancy. One of those faggy drinks."

Nellie shook her head but the waitress smiled and went away. Obviously she only had one master.

"I never run into anyone I know at the airport. Not anyone from back in the day anyway. Why's that?" Taz downed the rest of his drink.

"Because we only know poor people. And when you do well, you can't have poor friends. Not because you don't want to but because they don't call you up anymore. They run off to the States to become better people or they take off for butt-fuck Alberta and forget your number." Nellie fingered the appetizer menu. "Have you heard from Julie lately?"

Taz shook his head.

"Everett quit drinking," she added.

"Are you fucking with me? Drugs too?"

"I guess."

"I guess that explains some things. About two weeks ago, he calls me up and asks me where I am. I was in Vancouver. And what do you know he shows up a day later — "

"I thought he was in Arizona — "

"Apparently not. So he came to see me and said he had a message for me from the spirit world." Taz laughed.

"Are you fucking kidding?"

Taz shrugged. "Apparently some nosy spirit said I should return my dad to his resting place."

"You mean like dig him up and move his bones? Are you going to do it? Is that even legal?"

Taz sighed heavily. "Nellie, my dad is still alive. Why the fuck does everyone think that he's dead?"

Probably because it's hard to believe you ever had parents, Nellie thought. "That's true, I'd have probably heard over the moccasin telegraph if your dad died."

"Moccasin messaging these days." Taz wagged his cell phone, "Anyway I told the genius that and he said he was just the messenger. I told him he was fucked and to go have a beer."

"How did he look?"

"Oh dreamy, his muscles were so muscular." Taz laughed, "How the fuck should I know? He looked big and stupid as usual."

The waitress placed the drinks, smiled and went away.

"She's too beautiful to be working here."

Taz shrugged. "How long you staying where you are?"

"Forever I guess."

"'Til they bleed you dry."

"It's permanent Taz. I don't have to wonder where my paycheck is coming next year."

Nellie took a long sip of her wine. Wine tasted the same before noon.

Taz's face was dull and sweaty, some of his hair was plastered to his forehead. "How long have you been drinking?" she asked.

"A couple hours. Started on the plane. It seemed to be going well so I decided to continue."

"Where are you going?"

"Back to Vancouver — some conference, fisheries, treaties, reserve creation — one of those fucking things."

"You sound really committed. Ideal employee."

"They don't give a shit. As long as I show up for meetings with a brown face. And that I got. In spades."

"I worry about your soul."

Taz grabbed Nellie's hand and squeezed it. "I appreciate your concern." He laughed and grabbed his glass; Nellie noted a few blingy rings. They looked garish on his otherwise nice hands.

Taz raised his glass. "To money!"

A Caucasian couple looked in their direction; their expressions were horrified. Like Taz had yelled, "To bombs!" in the airport bar. But then again, to some white people, Indians having money was just as criminal.

"I'm not toasting to that."

Taz laughed, short and sharp. "I thought you liked to play along."

"Since when?" Nellie's wine was thin but not too sweet. It was perfect airport wine. "Have you heard from Julie?"

"You already asked me that. She calls me up once in a while and asks for money."

"Did you cheat on her?"

Taz flicked his dark eyes at her and Nellie felt a frisson of unease for asking what she thought was a fair question.

"Did she say that?"

"She never said anything. One day she was here and the next she was gone."

Nellie sipped her wine. Then took a bigger gulpy sized slurp as she stared at the people walking by. They looked busy and distracted, their thoughts on where they were going and how long it would take, on whether or not their luggage would make it.

Taz said, "Yeah, Indians got a way of disappearing.

"Like those guys they found outside the city. The ones the police dropped off."

"That happened to me." Taz was looking into his amber glass.

"Seriously? When? Did you report it?" Nellie would have gone straight to the press and told her story to a million microphones. She would have talked until all those cops were locked up and the key was thrown into the Saskatchewan River.

Taz slapped her questions away like annoying mosquitoes.

"I have to buy a suit," he announced.

"Why?"

"I lost my luggage."

Nellie didn't bother to ask how. She'd spent enough time around Everett to know that the odd and incredible happened with alarming regularity when you spent days at a time drunk. "There's the Bay. I guess. I don't buy men's suits. Can you wait until you get to Vancouver?"

Taz couldn't. He jumped to his feet, swayed for a second before catching his balance. He dropped a pile of cash on the table without counting it.

Nellie counted the bills hurriedly before following him. Taz didn't leave much of a tip so she made sure to drop a five as they left. *Who's your master now, bitch*, Nellie thought.

Taz grabbed her suitcase from her. "This is a pretty jazzy suitcase."

"I do love it."

"It's like it's a part of you." He twirled with it as he walked and Nellie had to smile.

They took a cab directly to the Bay. The store was empty of customers and the employees were cleaning the glass of their counters. Nellie felt like everyone knew that she was skipping out on work. Taz strutted with his customary short-guy-with something-to-prove walk.

They walked past the displays of shoes and Nellie looked at a few longingly.

"Why do women love shoes so much?"

"So many kinds, each shoe is for a different event and they just make you feel different I guess. Like you're ready to go anywhere."

"Women are vain."

"Right Liberace, like those rings aren't a sign of vanity."

"These were a gift from my father, they signify my lineage as hereditary chief of my territory."

"Really?" Nellie looked closer.

"As if. Fuck, they're just rings. I'm a fancy man."

Nellie's laugh was so loud it reverberated off the walls. She caught her reflection in a mirror, her mouth wide open, her eyes slightly insane. *Bring it down Nellie or you're gonna end up being escorted out by some pimply faced security guard.*

"What kind of suit do you need?"

"Grey. I like grey."

"Not black? You are the grim reaper, bringing death wherever you tread . . . are treading . . . treaded." *Jesus, Nellie, it was only one glass of wine. And it was a mild wine.* Nellie giggled.

"What are you cackling about?"

"Words, like the word 'mild'. You can take a word like mild and it minimizes everything, like a mild storm or mild insanity."

"Mild aggravated rape."

"Of course you had to go there." Nellie stopped in front of the men's area. The mannequins were the size of fifteen-year-old boys. The designers' ideal size, Nellie mused. She preferred her men tall, broad shouldered with a slight stoop, and a belly that was flat but soft because he didn't spend his life in a gym. Arms that were strong from carrying things that mattered. Hands that were callused and cracked because he worked with them all year long.

"Are you in love with that fucking thing?"

"He keeps his mouth shut which is a quality more men should have."

"And you're single? So hard to believe." Taz pulled a suit off the hanger and inspected it.

"What are you — a forty-two-short?"

He looked at her in surprise, "Do I look that fat?"

He wasn't skinny. But he did have a slightly athletic look to him. Some women might even like that powerful bullish look. Nellie didn't.

"You aren't fat."

"Neither are you."

"We're not talking about me."

"Yeah, but I wanted to say that. You've slimmed down.Like you got a waist and everything."

Nellie pretended to look at the ties. "Do you like patterns or solids?"

"I don't care. I guess I should try this one." He held up a slate grey suit.

"Looks good."

"Do I just take it?"

"You try it on bonehead." Nellie pushed him in the direction of the dressing room. "Call me when you're done."

"I don't show you. You're not my mom."

"Go."

He walked towards the dressing room, his head down and if Nellie didn't know better, she'd swear he almost looked uncertain, like a little boy. Nellie dismissed the thought; she was not going to feel sorry for Taz.

Nellie saw a dark head of long hair walking through the clothes and her head turned as it always did. It was only a tall woman. It had been two years since she'd seen him.She heard that he was in BC, then she heard that he was up north, she heard he went down south, that he was thinking of joining the army, then she heard that he didn't believe in the army and was trying to set up a warrior society, she heard that he was in Poundmaker's Lodge trying to heal himself, then she heard that he was seen at 49'er, making out with a Powwow princess.

Why couldn't she run into him at an airport sitting quietly in a Chili's? Because Everett would probably never fly. Even if he had the money, he would prefer to spend it on gas so that he could invite along a buddy or two and the trip would take at least a week longer than it needed to because that is how things were supposed to happen, you were supposed to enjoy your life.

I enjoy my life, Nellie insisted, *in a different way. Like I enjoy having nice stuff so I don't always invite the party over or invite relatives to stay who don't know how to leave. And I like my quiet so I don't go to parties all the time. I'm responsible so I can't devote myself to fun.*

Except on Monday mornings when she was wandering around a mall at 11:00 AM with a glass of wine under her belt.

Nellie stood at the door of the changing room. "Taz? You done? What's it look like? Taz? You need a second opinion on a big purchase, trust me on that. God I wish I'd had a second opinion when I bought those two hundred dollar shoes with the gold straps that cut into my ankles and gave me a scar." That was the longest amount of time she had ever spoken to Taz without being interrupted.

Nellie opened the door to his change room. He was asleep on the floor, his pants off, the suit jacket on. He wore jockey boxer shorts. Nellie was grateful for that. The next ten minutes were not going to be fun. Taz was a big man and Nellie was not that strong. Before she began the job, she paused to pull her digital camera out of her carry-on bag.

৵৵৵

He slept all day. Nellie worked at her kitchen table and wandered by the couch once in a while to check on his breathing. While he slept he turned to stone, his face hardening and taking on a grey cast. *Julie liked waking up to that face? She was a strange one.*

She leaned close to check his breathing. A reflex from when she was younger.

Mongoose-fast, Taz grabbed the back of her head and pulled her close.

It had been awhile so Nellie allowed herself to be kissed. Plus maybe she'd even wondered over the years, had looked at those lips across the table more than a hundred times. She tasted cigarettes, whiskey, a roast beef sandwich, and — she wouldn't have been surprised to find out that Taz had eaten regurgitated cat food. She broke off the kiss.

"No," she said leaning back on her butt.

"No?" Taz's eyes were half-closed.

"If you sweet-talked me, told me that I was the only woman you've ever wanted, that I am the woman that you dream of and that I come to you in your dreams enveloped in smoke like a girl in a music video, then . . . maybe."

Taz pretended to snore; Nellie laughed and went back to her desk.

When he woke up a few hours later, he ordered some Chinese food. He ate it with appalling speed. He wanted to go pick up some beer but Nellie distracted him with iced tea. They watched TV together or at least Nellie tried to watch but Taz kept talking to her about Native politics. Even though he worked for the feds now, he was still involved behind the scenes. Nellie hadn't paid attention. She saw the chiefs sniping at the government and at each other in the media — she found it embarrassing.

Taz had a different perspective, of course, having been raised at the teats of politics (his words). He was bitter about the direction that the Assembly of Saskatchewan Chiefs had taken. Nellie half-listened, thinking that keeping him sober had been a mistake.

"The real problem is that they've lost a connection to the grassroots . . . "

"Whatever that is."

"It's you, me, all the people back on the rez."

"As if they care what we think."

"What do you want?" Taz stared at her.

"Wine that doesn't stain my teeth?"

"Be fucking real." Nellie gave him a dirty look. He smiled, knowing he was annoying her.

"I guess . . . I see that our people are still getting arrested, locked up, committing violence or getting dumped by the side of the road — I see the young kids on the streets wandering — where are their parents? Why aren't they at home? — like how I was at home at their age, doing my homework, watching TV with my family . . . that's where kids should be. 'Cause pretty soon they're not kids anymore, they're adults and then we've lost them."

"Exactly." Taz pounded his fist on her coffee table and their iced tea jumped. Nellie reached for her glass.

"Okay, relax, Mandela."

"But that's what I'm talking about — we have to focus on the youth — on education and programs like sports and rec and make sure that our next generation isn't wasted. That's what those fuckers should be focussing on."

"Yeah. That would be good. But so what?"

"So everything."

Nellie looked at him. He was staring off into space or maybe at his reflection in the front window — he was that vain. She looked at his profile. With fifteen pounds off of him, stuffed into a good suit, better haircut — there was something there.

He kept talking and she started listening. By the time Arsenio was introducing his first guest, Nellie was ready to quit her job.

The Election

October 2004

Taz began most of his sentences, "When I'm grand chief . . . " no matter who the listener was, no matter how much Nellie tried to shush him.

"Nominations haven't even opened yet," she would hiss, "why give the competition a running start?"

But Taz never listened to the caution in her voice. Unlike Nellie, he didn't need to visualize or think positively, he knew that it would be and continued to stride into meetings and conferences with his cocky little walk and, God help her, Nellie began to believe it too.

So much so, that she invested in a few new suits even though her savings were moving faster south than a white pensioner. She had tried to keep her job with the government but after Taz went off about government deception destroying the intention of the treaties to a reporter . . . her boss politely hinted that a resignation might be in order.

The new suits weren't the investment she thought they would be. They caused her to get sideways looks from other Native women and murmurs of "ch, who's she trying to be?"

But Nellie was too cheap to buy different clothes. Besides the suits hid her growing midsection — she was getting chunky from road food and too much wine late at night.

She barely had time to miss her job, they kept such a fast pace. There were conferences, powwows, funerals, two weddings, a graduation and the Chiefs Assembly. Wherever First Nations were congregating, they were there.

Taz was a surprise to Nellie. For a horrible person with a terrible personality, he knew how to work a crowd. Women liked his smile; men liked his confidence. At large events, he would grab the mic and humbly thank the MC for inviting him to speak and the MC would nod and clap even though Taz hadn't even been invited to the event. He would give impromptu speeches that inspired, informed and most importantly, made people laugh. They weren't spontaneous. There were three standard ones that Nellie had written: education, justice and economic development with the right sprinkling of references to treaty rights.

Nellie looked after the details. She researched the issues and presented them to Taz. She looked at the legislation for the organization. There was a lot of it.

"It says here that anyone running has to have a clean criminal record for at least ten years."

"So what? I've got a clean record."

"It's crazy. The provincial election act doesn't require that, neither does the federal. "

"Like I always said, when you're an Indian, you gotta be ten times as good to get to the same place."

Once the nominations were made and accepted "oh so humbly", Nellie started researching their competition. It was a soft-spoken old man and a woman with a law degree. The old man had a history of bad financial management that was following him around like a skunk smell and the woman had blond streaks in her hair — nobody was taking either of them seriously.

"The only person who could beat me, is myself," Taz told Nellie in the car one day.

"I could," Nellie replied.

Taz laughed at that.

They shared hotel rooms for financial reasons. Nellie had only two rules: no smoking, no women. Taz only broke her rules a few times. So, more than once, Nellie opened the hotel room door to the sight of a half-naked woman running to the bathroom.

She wished he would get serious with someone. At formal events, sometimes he would put his hand on her shoulder or lean close to whisper in her ear. She allowed this so that people watching would make assumptions. Taz and her looked appropriate together, northern bush and southern rez, well-dressed, with money, about the same age. She figured it could only help his chances.

And besides, she knew it would move through the moccasin telegraph, down the road a few area codes. Sure enough one night when she was working in front of the TV, the phone rang and her heart leapt when she saw the number. She turned down the TV.

"What's shaking Nellie?" His voice was clear and bright — he wasn't drinking.

"I'm good."

"I hear Taz is gonna win."

"That's what they say."

"I'm coming home next week."

Home?

"You are?"

"Yeah, kind of getting tired of all this heat. I miss me some windchill."

Nellie laughed softly and curled her legs under her. Her eyelids felt heavy suddenly and her breathing slowed as she listened to him describe a night he spent walking through a desert looking for his wallet.

Taz was at her place when Everett showed up. Nellie was furiously working on a redraft of a brochure, on the phone negotiating the price of a hall rental and reviewing the invitation list for Taz's election party when Everett wandered in.

He didn't knock. He walked in the side door, and through the galley kitchen into the dining room — and she counted every step that brought him closer to her. He had a duffel bag over his shoulder, and wore a T-shirt that said Corona and a pair of jeans so old and worn, a strong breeze could blow them apart. Nellie beamed at him but didn't get up because she didn't want to disturb all of her papers. Taz jumped up from his chair and gave him a one-armed bro-hug.

"Where you been, man?" Taz asked.

"Tucson."

"What the fuck is in Tucson?"

"I went down there to work with a healer and I stayed until he finished teaching me."

Taz raised an eyebrow but held his tongue — Nellie knew he wasn't a fan of Everett's spiritual stuff. "How's the tail down there?"

"I wouldn't know bro. I was there to learn."

Taz's cell-phone started vibrating on the table and he mouthed the word sorry as he answered it and went into the other room.

"I should start supper," Nellie said, feeling naked and hot and fat all of a sudden.

"You cook?"

"I meant I should start to order something," she reached for her phone.

"Same old Nellie."

"Not quite the same, got some extra weight." She patted her tummy. "All this eating out is catching up with me."

Everett looked her over and Nellie felt her body heating up like a pizza pop in a microwave.

"Adds to the curves."

Thank God, getting all spiritual hadn't cut his balls off.

"Where you staying?" She asked in what she hoped was a casual voice.

"With a friend. Got some renters in Michael's house." Nellie didn't realize he knew how to get renters.

Nellie decided to take things slow. So she waited a week before asking him to move in with her. He surprised her by saying, "I don't think that's a good idea. If we rush, someone could end up getting hurt."

And we both know who the owner of the hurt feelings would be, Nellie thought ruefully. Despite that, Nellie instantly went into convince-mode. "I'm hardly ever home. We're always on the road and it would be nice to have someone in my place. For safety."

She was gone the first night he moved in but she imagined him in her bed and that made her smile. She didn't call him or anything, not because she didn't want to, but because every night she fell into bed and died. Taz teased her.

"So does your apartment lock from the outside or are you gonna shackle him to the bed this time?"

"Ha ha."

Everett would never commit of course. Unless he had changed. People grew up, didn't they? They matured and then they wanted the same things as everyone else. Or maybe they never did but then you adjusted to their unique way of thinking? She wanted to marry Everett and he never wanted to settle down and so she had to compromise. And he had to compromise. And the in between point was that he would live in her house and she wouldn't complain.

On one of their breakneck races from a Saskatoon conference to a Regina round dance, Nellie asked Taz, "Do you think I'm doing the right thing?"

Taz had to be reminded before he knew what she was talking about. He shrugged. "As long as you don't get all messed up and start balling your eyes out like a fucking pussy, I don't care."

When Nellie got home, Everett was there. He'd found a job. They celebrated by drinking a bottle of wine and making out on the couch. Before they could go all the way, he passed out. Or pretended to. Nellie walked her frustrated butt to bed and before she fell asleep made a complete list all the reasons she shouldn't love him.

A week later he lost the job. Then he found another one. It didn't pay as well but it had better hours and a nicer boss. So that was fine. He went to a different ceremony every weekend.

Nellie lost track of the names of Elders he mentioned and tried not to let her eyes glaze over when he described their teachings.

Sometimes they sat together on the couch while he drank a beer and watched TV and Nellie drank a glass of wine and worked. At bedtime, she went to the bedroom and he stayed on the couch. She was too afraid to ask him to follow her.

She laid in bed staring at the ceiling and wishing she had time to go to Pilates classes and get rid of her muffin top, narrow her butt and make her legs slender and long (the advertisements actually claimed that the classes could make your body into a professional dancer's body — it would be a nice change from a professional bowler's body). She could hear him snoring in the other room.

Overall, the situation was fine. Nellie could live with it. *Love takes time*, she reminded herself. Patience is a virtue. Her mother used to tell her that all the time and usually it sent Nellie into a rage, "I don't want to be fucking virtuous!"

One night when Taz and Nellie were working furiously at the kitchen table (technically Nellie was working while Taz was texting a girl that was way too young for him), Everett came over to check out what they were doing. While Nellie was explaining the focus on supporting young families, Everett rested his hand on her shoulder and said, "You need to rest Nellie."

So they would have continued inching along until fate intervened in the shape of a woman. The election was days away and Taz and Nellie were out late visiting different radio stations while media interviewed him. Nellie, proud as Dr. Frankenstein, looked on. *My monster is doing so well.*

They pulled into the drive, quietly buzzing on their own personal highs. Taz had almost left without going in but Nellie reminded him that they had to prepare for a 7:00 AM TV appearance.

As soon as they walked in the door, Nellie knew something had changed. It was the perfume in the air, the music turned up a bit too loud. Then Julie came around the corner. Taz, never one to hold back, picked her up and spun her around.

"It's good to see you," Nellie said when it was her turn but she was mad. Because she was a woman and she needed more than a hug. She needed an explanation.

Taz hadn't had a drink in weeks but this was a big night. He picked through Nellie's meager wine collection, dismissed it and then he and Everett headed out for some extra booze.

Nellie sat at the table and stared at some papers in front of her. Julie sat across from her and pretended that sitting in silence was normal. She picked up an election brochure.

"So, he's gonna win, huh?"

"Is that why you came back?"

Julie gave her a disapproving look.

"The timing is pretty suspect you have to admit."

"Why can't you ever just come out and call someone a cunt?"

"That's a disgusting word."

Julie laughed. "Maybe I came back for you? Maybe I came back for Everett?"

Nellie's heart stopped.

"Maybe I came back and it has nothing to do with any of you. Maybe sometimes I do things and there's no reason?"

"Maybe you only care about yourself?" And then Nellie's eyes teared up as they always did when she was mean to someone to she cared about.

She stood up and went to the kitchen. She tore a square off the Bounty roll and wiped her tears with it. As upset as she was, she noticed that they really did absorb moisture well.

"Don't cry Nellie."

That was a lost cause. "I get one call three years ago and then nothing. I would have reported you missing except Taz said you were asking him for money. I mean what the fuck? What did I do to deserve that?" Nellie blew her nose on the Bounty square and turned back towards Julie. She looked so small under Nellie's gaze. Her posture was still that strange mix of straight and relaxed; like a ballet dancer who smoked pot.

Nellie could see Julie retreating as she watched. Julie's eyes went flat. Nellie growled — she didn't want to scare her away — but what the fuck! Nellie turned on the faucet and filled a glass. She drank it with a shaky hand.

"I lost my baby." Julie said in a clear voice.

Nellie dribbled some water on herself. "What?"

Julie looked past Nellie, out the window. "A little girl. And I didn't deal too well with that, y'know?"

Jesus Christ, who would? Nellie ran the tap and poured another glass of water. She drank this one slower. She put it down harder than she wanted. She watched the water slosh back and forth. "Are you okay now?"

"Are you ever okay?" Julie had a lopsided smile.

"Do you want to talk about . . . your daughter?"

Julie shook her head, silent as the sun.

When the boys came back, Nellie gave herself permission to get boisterous. They did shots, they laughed, and they told stories.

"I had a lesbian experience last year," Julie said. All three heads swivelled in her direction.

"Bullshit," Nellie laughed.

Julie swatted her. "For real I did. I was really drunk this one night out in Hobbema. I don't even know how I got out there but there I was, at some party. Everyone was doing coke which kind of freaked me out — "

"Omigod you tell a story like an old woman," Taz groaned.

"Awus, just 'cause you're horny for the good part," Nellie shot back.

"Anyways, I got really drunk sitting in the living room, finishing off this bottle of Jack by myself. Next thing I know, I wake up and I'm eating some girl's snatch."

"What?!"

"Did you like it?" Everett asked.

"I realized what I was doing and I threw up. Like all over her pussy."

Everett and Taz were aghast.

Nellie roared with laughter. "Vomit in the snatch! What did she do?"

"She was pretty mad."

"You do not want puke in that area," said Nellie.

"Too hard to clean out."

"All those nooks and crannies," Nellie agreed.

Nellie and Julie killed themselves laughing. The guys were less impressed as they'd hoped for a different ending to the story.

The drinks kept flowing and more stories followed. Taz missed his TV appearance; when it was time to wake him, Nellie found him on the couch with Julie in his arms.

She walked back to the bedroom and climbed under the covers. She wriggled closer to Everett and inhaled his smell before her eyes grew heavy and sleep claimed her. She didn't even wake up when Everett slipped out of bed and into the morning.

The City of Lights

March 2007

NELLIE HAD A RIP-ROARING dream. She was in Paris with her mom and they were poor and ragged like those peasants in that movie that was based on a musical that was based on a book. They were searching for food because they were hungry and then at some point Nellie realized that she was pregnant. Pregnant in Paris with no money. That was a shitty scary dream.

"I thought you wanted to have a family," she mused, staring up at the ceiling at 3:30 AM. "Apparently not." But she did, she just wanted it on her terms, with a husband who would be a good father. She didn't want to be like those single moms she saw waiting at the bus stop in the middle of winter, struggling with their strollers, their heads wet with snow because they didn't have coats with hoods.

Nellie tried to go back to sleep. Failed. And so was out of the house by 5:00 AM standing in line grabbing a coffee. She almost smiled at a tall, nice-faced, silver fox but she couldn't see his hand to check if he had a wedding ring so she decided not to bother. It was strange though, before she hit her thirties, men with grey hair were invisible and now almost magically, they had appeared — to ignore her like every other type of man.

In the car she pressed her blinking message alert on her cell and listened to the first onslaught as she wove through traffic, always driving faster than everyone else, even though logically it didn't matter. They always ended up at the same red light where the driver would shoot angry looks at her while Nellie stoically stared straight ahead.

The messages were short. Lots of requests for call backs. Two of the calls were from chiefs and so her blood pressure immediately jumped.

Then three low priority calls, a councillor, an Elder and a provincial politician's assistant. The last call was from her mother reminding her of supper the next day and then finally her assistant calling in sick.

"Fuck."

Nellie closed the door to her office and fell into her chair.

She looked up again after noon. There were no meetings scheduled and Taz was out of town so she had the luxury of concentrating on a brief she was writing about the lack of policing services in northern communities. It would have been a perfect day except that her stomach was raging at her.

She hit her phone.

"Hey you eat already?"

"Nah." Julie's voice had sleep in it.

Must be nice thought Nellie.

They met a health food place that neither of them was crazy about. Julie never saw the point of eating healthy and Nellie only paid it lip service.

Nellie picked the sprouts out of her sandwich as she described a play she'd seen on the weekend to Julie. Julie nodded at the right spots.

"How was the date other than that?" Julie asked.

"He's really nice."

"And?"

"I don't know."

"Can you imagine sucking his dick?"

Nellie choked on her coffee and looked around before answering. "Jesus Christ no."

"There's your answer," Julie said.

"I need to date different kinds of guys. I can't only pick guys who are hot. That hasn't gotten me anywhere."

"Yeah, you need someone smart."

"Everett is smart, just not in a book way. Maybe now he is, I heard he's getting his GED or something. I dunno. Probably has a young girlfriend he's trying to impress."

Julie shrugged.

"She's probably naturally skinny and one of those free spirits who goes where the wind blows and her name is Aurora, or Skylar, or Shenoah."

"Shenoah?"

"And now all he does is talk about spirituality and getting to know the wisdom of the Elders and blah blah blah. He's even doing a Sundance ceremony this summer."

"That's cool."

Nellie sighed. "Guess it's better than him drinking himself to death. I want another coffee, you want a coffee?"

Julie shook her head. Julie did not cram herself full of things every chance she had. *Try to be content*, Nellie told herself. *Try to be grateful for that meal that you ate and did not taste.*

Nellie held Julie at the table for an extra half hour after they finished. "I don't want to go back to work," she moaned over and over again.

Julie told her about a class she was thinking of taking in early childhood development. Nellie didn't have the heart to tell her that the pay was ridiculously low and the hours were early and long. Because Julie wanted to be around kids and didn't give a shit about things like that.

Nellie studied Julie. There were dark circles around her eyes and she looked bonier than usual.

"You feeling okay?"

Julie nodded.

"Any more doctors?"

"We're taking a break. With work and the re-election coming up Taz doesn't have time."

Nellie had sent him to Ottawa the day before to argue for more funding from INAC: "Don't come back without at least another ten percent." She knew how busy Taz was. Still she wished he had made the time. Then again she knew how sensitive men could be about their dicks.

Julie blew on her coffee. "It bothers him though. I know it does."

"There's always adoption."

"It's not the same though, is it?"

"All kids are weird to me. Short, always asking stupid questions — and those enormous freaky-doll heads. We got it made if you ask me."

Julie smiled and stayed for an extra coffee that she did not drink.

Nellie worked until nine and then dropped files on her assistant's chair. A nice passive aggressive welcome back message for the morning. She made an internal note to start looking for another assistant.

It was dark outside and she kept her keys in her fist as she walked outside. She was always ready for an attack. She saw a man standing too close to her car and pulled out her cell. But he got into the car next to hers. Nellie relaxed and thought about the last time someone had been in the parking lot waiting for her.

She had recognized the lanky body before she even got close. His head was tilted to the side in that way she hated so much.

Hold your head up straight for God's sake. You're a man, not a nervous teenage girl.

"Nellie." His voice was a chinook that had finally made its way to the prairies.

She'd always daydreamed about that moment when he would come back to her. She played out her reaction in different ways. Some days she threw her keys and hit him in the face, the sharp edge of the keys scratching that perfect skin. Other times she ran to him and he picked up her and they did that movie-style romantic spin. Other days they had sex on the hood of her car (although that entire parking area was covered with surveillance cameras so realistically that was never going to happen).

That day, however, she walked over to the car. They talked. They went for dinner. The next morning she lent him some money. That was months ago and she hadn't heard from him since.

Stop thinking about him. He doesn't deserve space in my brain. He can live without me. That was the refrain tattooed on her heart whenever she thought of calling him afterwards. She would hold the phone and have his number up and before pressing send she would stare at the inside of her wrist. She had pretty delicate wrists. They were her best feature by a long shot. In the twenty years that she'd known him he had never mentioned them.

Nellie had no idea what he loved about her, if he had ever loved her. Maybe he liked that she had always been there for him like the sun in the morning and the moon in the evening. And now that she wasn't, his love was withdrawn.

One part of her liked to put things under harsh lights to counter the romantic in her. She ruined things with her expectations. She needed to see them for what they were. This she had learned. After the hundreds of times Everett had taken her heart and snapped it like a hollow piece of firewood across his leg.

Besides she was dating now. Twice in one month a man had spoken to her and then somehow it transformed into a coffee date, a dinner date, and these dates were still sort of going. She had options other than the long-haired nomad. *And a modern day nomad is a just a drifter,* she reminded herself.

And she had a trip to Italy coming up. It was one of those on the bus, off the bus things. She had already bought a hat.

Stuff was happening.

Then she had the Paris dream again. Once again she was in the City of Lights with her mom but this time her belly was big. They had to run to catch some bus that would take them out of Paris, back home and Nellie couldn't make herself run. "Go Mom," she kept saying. Because if her mom left then she could come back with help. But, of course, her mom would not leave her no matter how much Nellie yelled at her to go. Nellie woke up hungry.

She was eating a high protein diet that a trainer had recommended years before but she'd never followed. Then she read that being fit was eighty percent diet and twenty percent working out so she cancelled her gym membership and bought some protein powder.

She had a shake. It wasn't even close to satisfying. At her coffee place, she ordered a bagel to go with her coffee. She forgot to flirt with anyone.

Her assistant kept her eyes on her computer when Nellie walked in. When Nellie said good morning, her assistant replied in a cold voice. But her fingers were moving rapidly which was all Nellie cared about anyway.

There were three meetings that morning. Coffee. Danish (lemon). Coffee with cream. Date square (in the morning?). Coffee with cream and sugar (not fake sugar either). A short-bread cookie (it was dry).

She went to lunch with co-workers and had a salad. On the way back to the office, she picked up a bag of chips, the family size. Then ate and worked her way through the afternoon. Happy as a pig in shit.

Her mom called again about supper. Nellie picked the place. They served big portions.

At supper, her mom asked about her dates. Nellie made the men sound much hotter than they were, although she stumbled over their names. How had she forgotten about them already?

"I've been having weird dreams lately," Nellie told her mom. "You're in them."

"Mothers represent youth. Or nurturing." Her mother was always reading books about the occult and astrology and other things that Nellie scoffed at.

"Whatever it is, we're not doing well. We're in Paris."

"I've always wanted to go there."

"We'll go next year."

"Next year your sister is getting married."

"She'll find a way to screw it up."

Her mother sipped her coffee in silent agreement.

"I'll book the trip. Maybe Julie will be able to come. I'm a bit worried about her."

"Still nothing?"

"Nope. They probably can't. I don't know why they don't admit it to themselves and move on to other options. Adopt. Get a surrogate. God knows Taz can afford it."

"It takes time Nellie."

"Well, whatever. They're wasting it. Do you want dessert?"

Her mother didn't but Nellie could talk her into anything.

That night they were in Paris again. Her mother was trying to dig something out of the ground. A weed that she figured they could eat. It would be bitter, Nellie knew, but she was so hungry she didn't care. Plus the baby was hungry. Nellie could feel the baby's hunger pains. *It's too much.* She told herself. *Babies are too hard.*

She woke up and sunlight filled the room which meant she slept in. She reached for her phone and made an appointment to see her doctor. She thought about her condo. She might have to buy a townhouse. Maybe something with a yard. Kids needed that right? She felt weak and shaky like she'd drank too much the night before.

Her doctor snuck her in that day because she was a good patient. She was a few years younger than Nellie and her eyes drifted to Nellie's wedding hand as she asked questions. Her doctor wore a thick gold band with a sparkling diamond. *Lucky bitch*, Nellie thought for the hundred thousandth time.

In the parking lot outside the clinic, Nellie sat in her car. She always hated people who sat in their cars. It made them look suspicious. Or they looked like their lives were so utterly out of control that their car was the only place they could hide. She sat in her car for a long time figuring out where to go.

That night she did not dream.

Sundance

August 2007

SHE WAS SITTING ON the front steps of his house when Everett got home from the Sundance. He'd pierced. He felt his shirt sticking to the blood because the wound hadn't closed up yet.

She wasn't reading or on the phone or smoking. She was sitting there staring up at him.

"How long you been here?"

"Couple hours."

"I didn't know you were coming."

"Nellie mentioned you were on your way back from the States."

He opened the door. The house smelled like heaven.

"I made tea," she said. "And spaghetti and meatballs."

He collapsed on a chair and ate.

She asked him about the ceremony. When he asked her about Taz, she brushed her hair behind her ears. "It's not working." In response to his skeptical look, she added. "I'm looking for my own place."

And then, she turned the conversation back to him.

"You excited to be a dad?"

"Yeah. But I don't know how to do it. I asked the Elders about what I need to know."

She frowned. "Are you helping Nellie?"

He shrugged. "She says she doesn't need me."

Her frown deepened.

"Hey," he said softly. "You know that I always do what you guys want in the end." He scratched around the wound where it itched.

She reached across the table and put her hand on top of his arm. Gently her long fingers drummed on his skin. "You'll be a good dad," she said.

It was dark outside when he cleared the table. He brushed against her shoulder when he leaned over to grab her plate. She didn't move away.

In the old days, he would have offered her a beer. Now he had tea and water and juice and coffee. He missed the old days.

She made it easy for him. Around ten she yawned, threw up her arms and said, "You ready to hit the hay?"

He followed her into the bedroom tentatively like a kid half expecting a spanking. She walked to the bed and pulled off her shirt, her bra, her jeans. Then she climbed into bed.

She felt better than he remembered. Lean still, but softer. He always worried that life would make her too thin. He remembered seeing her mom in the city once and she looked like a hungry child.

"Do you ever think about your mom?"

"Yes," her voice was calm.

"What do you think about?"

"The good times."

He held her to his chest and she slept like that.

He woke up feeling cold. The blankets were down by his waist. He looked to his side almost expecting to see Nellie there but there was no one. Julie. He remembered and got up to see if her bag was gone. She was on the couch asleep, the light was on beside her, a book near her head. She didn't go straight to sleep then.

He went to the kitchen. In a lower cupboard was where he kept them. It was a black case, like those bags that doctors carry. It always made him feel like a strange professional. He opened it and the silver glinted at him. He grabbed randomly knowing that any of them would work.

Then he knelt beside her and began to cut. Her face was hidden and then it was clear. He picked up the hair and put it in a plastic bag. Then he picked her up and carried her back to bed.

When he woke up again, it was to the sound her voice, annoyed, coming from the bathroom.

"Did you have to cut it all off?"

He got out of bed and looked at her reflection. Her hair stuck out in unruly tufts and had a faint "escaped from a mental institution" aura. "Sorry."

She pushed him. "Fuck, Everett."

"It looks nice." He reached out to touch the back of her neck where it curled up.

She slapped his hand away. "That's not the point."

"You're not looking for a place, are you?" There was a growl in his voice.

Caught in a lie, Nellie would get huffy, even start attacking like a hypocrite. Instead, Julie looked away, a half-smile turning up one side of her mouth. Everett found this more annoying, to be honest. He hit the side of the doorframe with the back of his hand.

Julie flinched but did not turn around. She picked up a pair of scissors. "Why do you have so many pairs?" She met his eyes in the mirror.

"I sharpen scissors for hairdressers."

"Always the fox in the henhouse, hey?"

"I fell into it."

She cut quickly, confidently as if she could see what it should look like. The hair fell in clumps in the sink.

"Never cut my hair," she said. "But I guess every woman should go short at least once in her life."

He watched her start on the sides, evening it out. Then along the top, making it look more like a brush cut.

"I think I'm ready for the army," she grinned.

He went to the kitchen to make breakfast.

They laid in bed that night and stared at the ceiling.

"I could get you a job in one of the salons."

"That would be nice. Me and my freak hair."

"You're the most beautiful woman I've ever seen."

She said nothing.

He woke up around dawn and watched her while she slept.

"That's creepy," she said without opening her eyes.

"I wasn't looking at you vain one."

She opened her eyes and brushed her hand against her head. "Why so short Everett?"

He rested his hand on her head and stroked its velvety softness. "You're like a deer."

"I'll never understand you." This was something Nellie would say so he knew she was lying.

After breakfast, she threw her stuff into a bag.

His new scar hurt worse than ever and he liked how that felt. How it made him weak and kept him still.

"I want you to stay." He said, in case she hadn't figured that out in the last twenty-five years.

She nodded and traced his nose with her finger, then kissed him.

He didn't watch her leave.

A week later, he came home to a car in his drive way. A green Volvo. He went inside the house.

Nellie was spreading out some Chinese take-out. It was way too much food for two people. "Is the army coming?"

She laughed nervously. "I didn't know what you like so I got one of everything."

They ate and Nellie told him her work stories. She seemed to be having fun at work, working on stuff she thought was important. The office had been getting calls about "residential schools." While she explained what they were, and how kids were abused there, his thoughts went to all those moments in ceremony when old guys talked about the stuff done to them in those schools and some of those guys weren't old, they were young like him. He didn't say this though, he let her talk. She could barely keep still as she told him how she was convincing people to tell their stories to lawyers and stick it to the government and the churches. "Someone should start a law firm and handle these claims," she said.

"Why not you?"

"I work with Taz." She glanced at the cellphone on the table. "Besides I'd have to bring in other lawyers and y'know I don't work well with other people."

"You work with Taz, you can work with anyone."

"We're doing good things too." She started putting covers on the food.

"How are you feeling?" he asked her. He always heard people ask pregnant women that.

"Bigger, obviously," she said and cupped her breasts. They were a lot bigger.

"Do you feel him . . . her . . . ?"

She shook her head. "Too early for that."

They fell back into silence. Everett ate fried rice and wondered whoever thought of putting fried eggs in rice first.

Finally she told him what she came to say. "Julie gave me a call a few weeks ago. I want you to know that. Because it was her idea, so don't get all mad at me."

He nodded.

"She suggested, but like in that determined Julie way, y'know . . . I know you like your privacy but she was insistent and I mean really we do it all the time at the office. We have a woman who researches family trees and well, it's kind of funny that you never asked me yourself."

"Asked you what?"

"To find your mom."

He exhaled and wished for a smoke and a beer. "Fuck, Nellie."

"She's alive!" She exclaimed quickly.

"Where?"

"Montana."

He must have driven through it at least a dozen times the past few years.

"Way down there?"

"She married a rancher."

"She's doing okay then?"

"I barely talked to her but she seems all right."

"You talked to her!"

"I wanted to make sure it was the right woman . . . " She put her fingers in her mouth. Everett knew she did that to appear nervous. *Little shit.*

"You guys . . . " he got up and went to the sink, went to the cupboard, went to the bathroom then the bedroom, looking for something but not knowing what. Nellie used to compare him to an old dog when he did that at their house. Same old stupid Everett. He sat on his bed and his heart felt like it did when he used to wake up after a hard drunk, like a bird trapped in a metal drum.

Nellie stepped into the doorway. "She wants to talk to you."

He tapped his foot on the ground. Nellie's eyes went to it, she always studied him like a mouse.

"Are you excited?"

"I guess you have her number."

"Yeah. Do you want to call her?"

"Not right now."

"Why not right now?"

"I don't know."

"Just call her." She paused, "Sorry, pushy Nellie."

She went back to the kitchen.

Everett remembered the day he bought Nellie's wedding ring. He was in a pawnshop looking around when he saw it, and right down to the moment before he paid for the ring, he had his eyes on an electric guitar hanging on the wall. Then he heard his mom's voice in his head, "How you treat others is what you think of yourself." Nellie had never seen that ring.

He stood up from the bed. He caught his reflection in the window. He looked so old. He went back into the kitchen.

"Can I get the number?"

Nellie nodded, her mouth full of fried rice. She ripped part of the brown Chinese food bag and wrote out the number and laid it on the table. The numbers sat there looking at him next to: "Fast Delivery, No MSG."

They finished eating. Nellie's phone vibrated through the meal so much that Everett figured she was probably dating someone now. Then he remembered, *she's pregnant, idiot.*

It was dark when she left. Before she headed outside, she pressed that little button and her car purred to life. She paused to wave at him, that little excited wave that never fit her.

He stood in the kitchen window and watched her go around to her side of the car. Before getting in, she stood by the door and brushed her hair back with her hand. It was so thick and curly that her hand got caught for a second, then she pulled it free.

She was putting the key into the ignition when he opened the door.

The Ferris Wheel

September 2007

"**F**AIR'S ON." TAZ WAS staring at the TV, the remote in his hand. He'd been home less than twenty seconds.

"I saw the parade on TV this morning."

"We should go. Eat some bad food, go on some rides?"

"I've been craving fries."

"Let me shower first then we'll go."

Julie put on a sundress. When she bought it, she thought it would be the perfect thing to wear to a fair. But when she saw herself standing in the mirror, it looked wrong. She always felt like a man in a dress, her shoulders looked too wide and her narrow hips got lost in full skirts. Dresses were something you had to have practice with, she decided. She pulled out a pair of shorts, then couldn't decide on a shirt to wear with it. Finally she put on a pair of jeans and a plain T-shirt. She used to wear only concert t-shirts but she was too old for that now. Simple was what grown-ups did.

Taz strode into the bedroom, his hair thick with water. Once it was wet, it took forever to dry. He looked her over, paused slightly on her face, before pulling his T-shirt over his head. While he put on his jeans, she reached for her make up bag.

Maybe she didn't have to walk around with a naked face all the time. There would be teenage girls there. *The bane of our existence*, Nellie had said the other day. Julie had laughed but then she started noticing them. Their skin: fair, plump and luscious. Their bodies crammed into shorts and tank tops carelessly showing off their smooth, gravity-defying curves.

Fucking Nellie.

Julie put on a layer of mascara, then another. Then smoothed on some lip-gloss. A brightened woman stared back at her. It looked like the same face she'd always seen but it was hard to notice time on your own face. That's what friends were for.

Julie hesitated at the door — jacket or no? She decided in favour of free hands.

They listened to a talk radio show on the way. One man moderated as two men discussed how much money the "Indians" wasted in this province. Julie hated listening to it but Taz liked to know what the "enemy" was thinking.

The fair parking lot was crammed full of cars. Taz drove around and around the parking lot trying to get as close as possible but still wanting to maintain distance between his car and everyone else's.

"It's not going to happen Taz." Julie said, adding a sigh where perhaps a sigh wasn't necessary.

"I didn't want you to have to walk far."

Julie held up her foot. "Flats, see? I'm a practical woman."

He put the car into reverse and backed down the road. Julie watched their progress in the rear view mirror. Taz was a very good driver; precise and controlled but maybe a bit too fast.

Julie heard the sounds of kids screaming when he got out of the car. Then the rattle of the roller coaster. Taz stretched in front of the car.

"Wait." She sprayed his back with mosquito juice.

It was the small things that made a relationship. Julie had seen that on Oprah. Or maybe she made it up. Probably she heard Nellie say it.

He grabbed her hand as they got close to the gate. Their hands were the same size, which made sense because they were almost the same height. When they were first dating he used to call her, "my giraffe," which she liked.

As he paid their entrance fee, Julie glanced at the families trudging out. Moms, sweaty and harried. Dads, red-faced, walking slightly ahead, looking back impatiently: "Hurry up." Moms yelling back: "Why don't you help me!" Children whining, and caramel apples everywhere. She grinned.

Taz led her towards the midway. Carneys called out to them. "Hey there, win a bear for your angel!"

Taz elbowed her, "They're talking to you."

Julie rolled her eyes.

Taz stopped at the gun game. The carney hurried up to them, "Five for a small, twenty for a large!" The guy had a lisp. Julie wondered how he had gotten control of such a big game. She imagined the struggle he must have faced to get where he was.

She imagined him standing up to the boss, those awkward few nights before people started believing in him, then victory as he overcame prejudice by having a few successful nights. She smiled to herself, more likely he was the boss' nephew.

She leaned against the game and watched as Taz shot the hell out of the star. The carney wasn't happy as he pulled the paper off the clip. The star was obliterated.

"You a hunter or something?"

"Why? Is it against the law now to win this stupid game?"

"Not many people can shoot like that."

"Give me my fucking prize."

The guy looked like he was gonna cry. Julie turned away.

She stared at the Orange Julius stand behind them. She walked closer to inspect it. Who bought Orange Julius anyway? It was just orange juice, why was it so expensive? Were they paying extra for the pulp?

"What are you looking at?"

He had a gorilla under his arm. It was the size of a ten year old child.

"We have to carry that thing around?"

"We should go on some rides."

He led her into the crush, she trailed behind him trying to dodge the bodies coming at her.

Guess my weight. Guess my age. Guess my job.

A child screamed, a boy, about four years old. His face was red with frustration. He held his hands up, signalling his desire to be comforted. A woman knelt in front of him.

A group of Native teen girls, heavy on the eyeliner, laughed into their hands about something only they would understand. The prettiest one noticed her and gave her a lookover. *At least someone was looking.* Then one of the girls noticed Taz and called out, "grand chief!" He wagged his finger at them, "Stay out of trouble!" and they giggled.

Women sat on the stools at the bingo table. They weren't playing, just fanning themselves with the cards.

When Julie was a kid she used to stand by the bingo game waiting. The guy who ran the stand wouldn't let kids sit down. He said the seats were only for players. Sometimes she got so tired she would sit on the ground. She'd watch people walk by with fries and she thought about running past them and stealing them out of their hands. But she never did it because she wasn't a fast runner.

"I could get fries right now."

"What did you say?"

"You want some fries?"

"I wanna go on some rides. We can eat after."

"Okay."

He bought some tickets. Too many, Julie figured as she held the giant ape. It was heavy. It wasn't going into her house, she knew that much at least, and would be in the garage before the week was through.

They went on the roller coaster. Taz chose the front seats. As the car rode towards the top, Julie looked down and saw the giant ape standing next to the carney.

"Kind of crazy, huh?"

"You can see a lot from up here."

"You can almost see our house."

"Few years we got to get out of there."

"Yeah?"

"It's on the wrong side of town."

The car passed over the crest and then anxiously rushed back towards earth. Julie's neck went one way, then the other, her hair swished across her face like car wash brush.

The car stopped with a jolt that Julie could feel right through her body.

"We should go on again."

"Okay."

They rejoined the line. He started talking to the teenage girls in front of them. He pretended to make the ape talk in a British accent. The girls were killing themselves laughing. Julie leaned on the metal fence around the ride. She balanced her hand on the top of the railing and rubbed it there.

The next time around, she only noticed the air on her face. It was hard to breathe. "I don't know what happened that time but it got my heart racing crazy-like."

She bent over and took some deep breaths.

"Jesus Julie, you're getting old."

Julie turned away from him. She looked across the fairway, at the crowds of people and felt their tiredness moving across her like a cloud. A blue jacket caught her eye. Dark denim like one she had at home. It was a skinny Native kid watching the crowd. Then, when he thought no one was looking he reached into the garbage bin beside him. He was poking through the food. He pulled out a tray of fries and began to eat them.

"Taz."

"What?"

"That kid is eating from the garbage."

Taz watched the kid shove the fries into his mouth like someone was gonna snatch them away. Taz walked over slowly like a hunter. The kid looked at him sideways, a foot poised to run. Taz said something. The kid laughed. She watched as Taz handed the kid some money and a bunch of tickets. Then he offered the kid the gorilla. The kid looked hesitant — it was really big and a pain in the ass to carry — but he took it anyway.

Taz had a big smile when he got back to her.

Julie gave him a peck on the cheek. Some drunk idiot woohed.

"I got ten tickets left. What ride you want next?"

"Ferris Wheel?"

Taz counted out the tickets and handed them to the carney, a wan-looking girl about sixteen. She looked like she didn't have the muscles to open the door much less run the ride.

Julie grinned as Taz let her slide in first. "This was my favourite ride at the fair when I was a kid."

"Not me, I was always on the zipper."

"I like how far you can see. And it always goes the longest."

"Where's the office?"

"We're facing the wrong direction."

Taz turned behind them; the cart shook.

"Taz, don't do that."

"I knew I could scare you."

She laughed and hoped that was the end of it.

The wind hit them at the top. The cart lifted up and then floated back again. She shivered.

"You cold?" Taz took off his jacket and handed it to her. Julie leaned her head on his shoulder.

Taz kissed the top of her head.

"I went to the doctor today."

"Why?"

"To get that mole burned off my neck."

"Good, that thing was gross."

Julie laughed. "Anyways, 'cause I was there already, we decided to do a pregnancy test." She searched his face.

"And?" She couldn't read him; could she ever?

"It was positive."

Taz frowned. "For real?"

"Aren't you happy?"

"How many months?"

"Not sure. Maybe two?"

They went down and came back up again.

"You're not happy?"

"I'll be happy when it's born. Right now you're another thing to worry about." He put his hand on hers.

She nodded.

The wind gusted again and Julie reached up with her free hand to brush her hair out of her eyes. She let it move downwards to her eyebrow and felt that little dent. Nobody knew it was there except her. *Nobody expects you to be perfect*, she reminded herself, but it bothered her.

"You wanna go again?" Taz had some tickets left.

"No, once is enough. Fries?"

"You got a one-track mind tonight."

She smiled and led the direction to the fry cart.

He tugged her arm. "I dunno, babe. I gotta watch my weight."

"They're for me."

"Go get them then, Chubs."

She stopped. Then restarted herself. Fries, fries, fries, fries. She weighed the same as she did when she was fifteen. All the women in her family were bony like that. Until the day she died, they told her that her mom looked like a boy from behind. She got to the cart and reached for her wallet. She remembered then seeing her wallet lying on the dresser with that raggedy five-dollar bill stuffed in its folds.

The man in the cart smiled down at her. "Watcha want, honey?"

Julie stared up at him. She had a feeling — totally crazy of course — that if she looked beside her, she would see a dark head of hair, slightly uncombed, a tiny face tilted upwards, hopeful that someone would be kind.

The Baby Shower

November 2007

"**Y**OU'RE LATE," NELLIE INTONED at the front door. Her face was still covered with the acne that started the day she got pregnant and continued through the nine months. "Everyone else gets a glow, I get a grease stain," Nellie would say.

Julie saw a wet mark down the front of Nellie's T-shirt, near her left breast and tried not to stare at it.

Taz pushed his way past Nellie dragging Julie behind him.

"This one had to run around town trying to pick up another gift for your kid — and some stupid cupcakes, do babies even eat cupcakes?" Taz went into the kitchen. "Do you have any beer?"

Nellie's eyes went to the cupcakes in Julie's arms. "Thank you," she said robotically. A glass smashed in the other room. They both flinched. "There are a lot of people here. I wish I hadn't let my mom plan this."

Julie patted her on the shoulder. "Where's the baby?"

"With my mom in the bedroom."

"How is Natalie?"

"She wants to be called Gammy. Sounds so dumb."

Julie raised her eyebrows and went to the bedroom. Julie could hear Nellie's feet shuffling behind her.

He was dressed in an Oilers hockey jersey with tiny sweatpants and shoes. His face was red.

Julie stopped in front. She ran her finger over his forehead and down his soft, protruding cheeks. "So chubby."

"Very," his grandmother said proudly. "Big already."

"Like his fat mom," Nellie leaned against the wall.

"Shut up," Julie said sharply. "Your son's a month old. Give yourself a break for God's sake."

"And change your shirt, you look nuts." Natalie added.

"Jesus I have a baby and everyone thinks they're the boss of me."

Still, she walked into her closet and closed the door.

"She's not sleeping well," Natalie explained. "I keep trying to get her to sleep. But she thinks she's supposed to do everything."

Everett and Taz walked in. Both of them had beers going.

"You're drinking?" Julie asked. Nellie had been so proud that he hadn't drank through the whole pregnancy.

"Like a fish." Natalie said sharply.

"Just celebrating," Everett said and knocked his beer against Taz's, who wasn't ready.

Taz's beer spilled down his shirt. "Oh for fuck sakes." He looked at Julie — she handed him a towel lying on the dresser.

"What about your mushum? Didn't he ask you to quit?" Julie watched Everett shift his weight from side to side, like a kid too shy to ask for the bathroom.

"No willpower." Natalie spit out.

"Yup," Everett agreed. "Hey little man." He swooped in and took the baby from Natalie's reluctant arms.

Taz inspected him. "He's a bruiser."

"Fuck, yeah."

"Support his neck," Natalie snapped.

Everett rolled his eyes.

"Can I hold him?" Julie asked.

Everett handed him over. He was heavy; a solid, strong little baby. He stared up at Julie; his eyes intense like his mother's.

"Hello," she whispered. "I'm your auntie Julie."

She sat down on the bed and shut them all out. She heard Natalie needling Everett about child support; she heard Taz asking about the game; she heard Nellie come out of the closet and chase everyone out — "You left my guests alone in the living room!" But she didn't take her eyes off of Malcolm. An old fashioned name. She liked that. She hoped no one ever called him Mel or gave him some stupid nickname that lived with him for his entire life like people did on the rez. She knew a guy who had been called "Poop monkey" since he was five years old. And then there was Taz. Hardly anyone knew his name was Nathan.

Julie watched his chest rise and fall, so much effort to stay alive. She wished they could jump forward in time until he was less fragile.

"I stopped nursing," Nellie said. "He was killing my nipples."

Julie nodded.

"I hate changing diapers. Maybe it's because he's a boy but they are super-gross. It's all soft and runny — like the worst ice cream flavour ever."

Julie laughed.

Nellie held out her arm. "Look at how my veins are all sticking out. My doctor says they'll go back in but what the fuck — whoever heard of that happening?"

Julie shrugged.

"And my stomach looks like a deflated balloon," Nellie was on a roll. "I stuff it into my pants. Like I thought I knew what a pot-belly looked like before, but this is . . . Hello?"

Julie looked up and smiled. "I've fallen in love."

"Oh well, that's okay."Nellie sat on the bed beside her. "Totally understandable."

◌◌◌

There was a cake in the shape of a car. The adults stood around it and thought about what they should sing. One of Nellie's friends said that there wasn't actually a song for baby showers.

Julie held Malcolm for most of the time, which meant she had to walk through everyone so that they could get a look at him. She was being greedy but couldn't stop herself and the only person who could have stopped her was eating cupcake after cupcake with mechanical precision.

"When do you want to leave?" Taz asked her.

"I want to help clean up. You can go."

He sighed, shrugged and went and grabbed another beer from the fridge. He joined Everett standing on the balcony.

"I love your hair," a young, blonde woman told Julie.

"It's so edgy but it works on you," said an older woman.

Nellie looked up from her cupcake. "You should have seen it before she cut it." A bit of icing was on the corner of her mouth. "At least this haircut brings her down to mortal status."

"You look like a movie star," the blonde woman insisted.

Julie's arms were killing her by the time she handed Malcolm over to his grandmother. She was about to plop herself on the couch when she felt a pain in her belly out of nowhere. *Liar, you've been ignoring that ache all day.* She walked to the bathroom and pushed the door open. She stood there without turning the light on.

How bad is it? I'm not a doctor. Then go to the doctor. I can't.

Last time, she was in the hospital. It was nurse who told her what had happened. She asked for the doctor and he delivered the news again in a heavily accented voice: "The baby is gone." And then after Julie's prodding, "A girl." Her girl had gone. It sounded so gentle like she had left for the library or went swimming with her friends.

This time she had worked things out in her head. If it was a boy he would play hockey with Nellie's son. If it was a girl, she and Nellie would fight over dressing her and doing her hair. Julie had imagined a closetful of cute clothes. She imagined that little hand in hers.

She felt tears on her cheeks and brushed them away.

The hardest thing in the world would be staying still. But she did. Even as people knocked on the door, she remained where she was, one hand on the wall, the other on the counter in front of her. She didn't even dare to use her voice. The pain came in waves and she breathed them away.

There was a knock at the door. "Are you sick?" Nellie's voice was raspy. She really was tired. Probably fighting off a cold.

"Yeah."

"Did you eat anything?"

"No."

"Everyone left. It's just me and the baby and my mom — well, Gammy — here."

"Taz?"

"Went for more beer with Tweedledum."

Julie took a deep breath and then another. She turned on the light. Surprised for a second to see her short hair, like a male version of her staring back.

Be brave. She pulled down her panties. She leaned close looking for a drop of anything. Nothing. She buttoned herself back up. Looked back at the strange woman looking at her. *It will be okay* she told her.

She opened the door.

Nellie looked her over. "Did you fall asleep in there?"

"I had the shits."

Nellie laughed. "Oh. Well. Hope it wasn't the cupcakes 'cause I ate like five."

"Do you want to go somewhere?'

"Not really. I want to take a nap. For like a few . . . years."

"That sounds good."

Julie watched Nellie sleep with Malcolm in her arms. He wound his fist around her finger. He was so strong already. Was that Everett? Or was that Nellie? But Nellie had never been much of an athlete. Malcolm frowned at Julie as if he could read her thoughts. "Now that is pure Nellie."

She could hear Natalie in the kitchen, humming softly, as she put everything into its proper place.

The Stars

February 2008

THERE WAS A BENCH in front of the Native Friendship Centre. He liked to go there early in the morning, with a tray full of coffees. People would come and talk with him:

"Chief, when you talk with the province, you should . . . "

"Gotta do something about those cops . . . "

"They got the guys piled on top of each other in the jails . . . "

"There's no jobs . . . "

"My grandkids — they went into care . . . "

"How do I sue the government . . . "

"I never met my mom . . . "

"My reserve won't help me . . . "

"The doctor says they're gonna take my leg, the whole thing this time . . . "

And, of course, "How about them Riders?"

And he would listen. For some, he would follow with a text to someone that he thought could help. Mostly he handed out twenties. "You're only making the problem worse," Nellie would tell him. But he didn't think so. Sometimes all someone needed was a little piece, not the whole cake.

Around nine, he'd gulp down the last of his coffee and shake hands.

"You're doing a good job."

"Don't let the bastards get to you."

"Don't take it personally."

"You can do it."

He climbed into his truck. Nice one, black 4x4, good on the rez roads. The kind he'd dreamed about owning when he was a kid growing up in Crow's Nest. Imagined it parked beside the road when he walked into the bush. Been a long time since he'd gone hunting. Been a long time since he'd gone home. Old Sam had called him the other day. Just to shoot the shit, ask about his old friends who were Senators and Elders now. Taz would describe meetings with them that may or may not have happened, making the stories funny for his dad. Then when Sam was happy, he'd call for Taz's mom; she never came to the phone. Wasn't a fan. Told her stories in letters that found him wherever he was and always ended the same way, "I am waiting for my grandchild."

Not long now Kokum. Julie was coming along. He turned around the other day in the bathroom and bumped into her tummy. They both laughed. Her size surprised both of them. Nobody else could tell though. That's how skinny she was normally. Not him, belly kept growing and growing, making him spend more on clothes than he wanted to.

His phone started buzzing.

"What's up?"

"Meeting with the Premier this morning." Nellie was talking through something in her mouth. Probably a donut. He'd told her to start losing the baby weight. But she never listened. Other chiefs had cute little things by their side. Maybe he should hire another assistant? One to travel with him.

"I'm on my way."

"I should be there."

"Its not that kind of meeting."

"Some kind of circle-jerk?"

He laughed. She could be gross like a guy. He liked that.

"They want it off the books."

"Do you have the Act?" She was referring to her baby, *The First Nation Child Welfare Act* — "protecting our children, our future" was the tag line she had for it.

"No. It's not that kind of meeting."

"But what if he asks for it? I should come drop off a copy."

"He has people who read things like that for him."

"But of course you've read it right?" She laughed. "As if."

He did try to read things. "Gotta go."

"Be careful."

"Awus." He hung up shaking his head. She was a fearmonger, that one.

They were meeting at a clubhouse on the city golf course. As he walked to through the clubhouse, he saw the snow on the grounds and wondered how long until he'd be able to dust off his golf clubs. The meeting was in the back of a backroom. Rooms he hadn't known existed were opening up for him all around the province. The trick was pretending that you knew they were there all along.

Four white guys stood up when he entered. *Damned if Nellie wasn't right.*

∽∽∽

They picked him up in front of a 7-Eleven. He had a liter of coke tucked under his coat. The blue and red lights flashed the second he walked out the door.

If I had stayed inside one minute longer.

They both got out of the car. Walking tough the both of them. One was about thirty-five; the other probably closer to forty. Mustaches, one with a bit of beard. They asked for his ID. He rummaged through his pocket. Found his wallet. Tried to balance the pop while digging through his wallet with one hand. His hands started to tingle in the cold air.

It was a five-minute walk, from his friend's shitty apartment to the 7-Eleven. "I'm heading out for mix 'cause you dumbass Indians don't know how to plan for nothing." He had thrown over his shoulder as he left the apartment. Didn't even bother to bring his gloves or hat.

The pop slipped from his arm and fell on the ground. It bounced once and then burst, the pop spraying over the parking lot, the sidewalk and the shiny black of their boots.

Arms were on him and Taz didn't struggle. There were two of them — and a trip to the drunk tank wasn't any reason to end up with a dozen shitty charges and a broken jaw. He glanced over his shoulder at the 7-Eleven. Nobody was watching.

∽∽∽

In Indian politics, the chiefs and councils voted for the grand chief. The people voted for the chiefs and councils. And if you pissed off your electorate then you paid bloody hell. But Taz had noticed that whites thought chiefs were like kings. Like he was the king of all the Indians. It was wrong — but he let them think that. Because if they didn't — then why meet with him?

There was an offer on the table. Nellie's Act had caught their attention. Native kids in care were not a good look for the province and things happened to them all the time. "We'll give you jurisdiction." The premier said.

"Acknowledge our jurisdiction." Taz corrected him.

"We'll recognize the Act." The premier waved his hand over Nellie's baby. "We won't stand in your way."

Taz waited. There was still a paper facedown on the table. The guy on the premier's left turned it over. Taz could read the words on there. They wanted their provincial sales tax. Something the chiefs would never agree to.

The premier cleared his throat. "We'll respect your jurisdiction on reserves of course, but off reserve, it has to be this way."

"How much are kids worth, right?" Taz said. His laugh sharp in the quiet room.

⪦⪦⪦

They went in the opposite direction of the cop shop. It took Taz a few minutes to realize that.

"Where are you going?" He asked.

They didn't answer.

He knocked on the window. "Hey, where you taking me?"

They were talking to each other, so he kept hitting the window between them and him. Then one of them slammed on it with his baton. "Fuck off."

Taz leaned back in the seat. He looked out the window. Were his friends wondering where he was? He and Everett had been drinking most of the day at their friend's place. They'd left the girls at home. Everett might think he went home. The girls would think he was with Everett.

There were no witnesses. Just the stars.

Taz's foot flew up and he started kicking: the window, that little plastic barrier keeping them away from him, the ceiling, even. If they were gonna kill him, they'd have questions to answer about dents in their roof and footsteps on the glass. More questions the better: Taz unzipped his jeans.

❧❧❧

He could have called Nellie. There was time. They even said he could think about it. "Take your time." The premier said.

Time for what? Time to go his chiefs and have them reject it? Like they had every other time the province had tried this?

There was a lawyer on the right side of the premier. Taz could tell by his suit and the pissy look on his face. The confidence that the law was always on his side. "It will happen. Whether you agree to it or not, it will happen."

So if I don't, you get the money, and the children, and we get the pride of knowing that we stood up to you.

He could have called Nellie.

Instead he signed.

❧❧❧

They stopped the car. Came around to the back. He held his legs up as the door opened and greeted the older one with a kick. It grazed his shoulder and Taz aimed with his other foot but the other guy had his hands on him.

"What the fuck?" One of them asked.

"Fucking animal."

They threw him to the ground and started putting the boots to him. He'd seen it happen to guys before, the dull thuds of the boots on a human body. It looked painful and it felt worse. He put his hands over his head and his face, hoping to protect himself from a brain injury. *If I can just get out of this.*

"You smell like piss."

"Dirty fucking Indian."

He could tell they were scared. His DNA in the car — his body bruised — his clothes all marked up. What kind of story were they going to make up to fix this?

One of them went back to the car. "What are you doing?" The young one asked. He turned his head towards the car and Taz seized his moment. He got up and ran.

His feet felt slow on the soft snow and so he moved towards the frozen stuff. There must be water near. *Where's the bush? Where's the fucking bush?*

He could hear footsteps behind him. So fast. Those fuckers worked out. But they had on big boots and big jackets. Taz was wearing sneakers and a light jacket. He heard a big sound behind him, one of them had slipped. He didn't look back.

⊰⊰⊰

Nellie was at her desk when he walked in. Technically it was his desk but she worked there more than he ever did.

He told her the good part first and saw a huge smile take over her face and light up her tired eyes. She was pretty when she smiled. He even got to see an excited little clap before he had to tell her the other part.

She jumped up, sending papers and pens flying. "Why didn't you take me? I told you not to go alone."

"It wouldn't have made a difference."

"You don't know that. I understand how they think, I could have threatened them with a lawsuit or bad press or something."

"They were going to do it anyway."

Nellie walked out from behind the desk where she sat six days a week, where she wrote letters and reports with "Protecting the Treaties," emblazoned across the top.

"I have a headache." She said near the door. Taz knew he should say something, something to convince her that it would all be okay. He said nothing and the door banged shut behind her.

Taz knew his day was just starting. He started dialing. Better the chiefs hear it from him.

᪉᪉᪉

Everett opened the door the next morning. He was shirtless, a string of hickeys around his neck. *Nellie would be pissed.*

Taz could see the shock in his face and knew he looked like hell.

"Taz? What the fuck?" Everett dragged him inside.

The warmth of the house felt painful. His skin pricked and stung as it came back alive.

"What the fuck? Who jumped you?"

Taz tried to talk but his face was too frozen. He stared up at Everett, so fucking glad to see someone he knew.

Over his friend's shoulder, he could see his reflection in a mirror. His face was white like a ghost, his eyebrows hairy with frost, his lips were grey. He looked dead.

But dead men don't cling to their friends. Dead men don't cry.

The Fight

JULIE PUT ON A blue top and tied the bow underneath her boobs. She caught a glimpse of herself as she walked out of the bathroom and sighed. Grown women should not wear bows. She could imagine younger Julie laughing at her.

Maternity clothes made her stomach look like a balloon. But she didn't mind that so much. What she minded were the enormous tits perched on top of it. She probably got stopped at least twice a day by men who wanted to offer her congratulations while staring at her breasts with an intensity that she worried would make them explode.

Julie took another look around the closet. There was nothing else. She had to go shopping again and made a mental note to ask Taz for more money. He hadn't minded shelling out for clothes the last few times she'd asked. They went to a lot of events these days with even more on the horizon as the election got closer.

She heard a beep outside and grabbed her purse. The fringes bounced against her hip and she was reminded of her mom. Her mom used to wear a light brown-fringed vest, like something a child would wear. Julie walked up to the picture on her wall; she was older now than her mom has been when she died.

When Julie got outside, Nellie had her butt hanging out of the backseat of the car.

"Someone got poopy on the car ride over." Nellie called out from the other side of her rear end.

"Shit happens," Julie commented as she settled herself in the front seat. She turned and grinned at the little boy lying on his back on the car seat. "Hi little man." He laughed in response. "He's so happy all the time."

"He's not a wriggler. Thank God, or I'd be fumigating this car every week." Nellie said as she taped the diaper in place. "You have to be really careful with the straps by the way, if they're loose, poop will leak out the sides."

"Hard learned lesson."

"The worst." Nellie strapped the baby into his car seat and by the time she climbed into the front seat, she was sweating. She collected her hair into a bun and tucked it under. "Everett was supposed to babysit but he got a job interview."

"Really?"

"Yup, at ASC. Sports coordinator. He's a bit old for a coordinator job but it's kind of ideal for him."

"He does love sports."

"And it'll get him out of the house. I get sick of him always being home." Nellie put the car in gear and started pulling out.

"How much money does Taz make?"

Nellie laughed. "Always blunt you."

"Yeah, well. I'm curious."

"Finally getting practical, are we?"

"I just want to know."

"I don't work in Finance — "

"Yeah, but you know."

"I don't know the exact amount but we're talking low six figures."

"Holy shit."

"He still giving you an allowance?"

Julie folded her hands on her belly.

"Why don't you tell him that grown ups don't get allowances — "

"Ha."

Malcolm made a little growling sound and Nellie patted his car seat with her free hand. "Remember when you used to steal food from the grocery store — that time you stole a whole roast — and even went to the till and paid for some bananas — "

"Yes I was thief. People grow up."

"I'm not saying it was a bad thing. It's just — you were fearless back then."

Julie didn't know where Nellie got that idea, she'd been scared shitless her whole life.

∽∽∽

After supper, Julie scrubbed the pots in the sink. She looked up and saw her reflection. Her hair had a soft curl she'd never seen before. While she wondered at it, she saw a dark head enter behind her.

"How was Nellie today?"

"She was good. Everett had a job interview."

"I know I saw him. 'Bout time, eh?"

"You think he'll get it?"

"Is that my T-shirt you're stretching out?"

"Sorry. I'm running out of stuff."

He grabbed a pop from the fridge. He was trying to drink less booze these days. It didn't look good when you were chief, he told her. Times were changing from when chiefs could party. If you have even a single beer then the gossip would be that you were a drunk. People were always looking for something.

The pot was gleaming but she kept scrubbing. Maybe she'd wait until he was ready for bed. Just before they had sex — that was a good time, right? Or after when he was relaxed? Or maybe in the morning? No Taz wasn't a morning person.

"I was wondering . . . " She heard the words coming out and wished she could call them back.

"What?"

"I have a lot of stuff to buy for the baby and I don't want to keep asking you because you're busy and I mean there's a lot of stuff."

"Like what? They drink milk and shit. And you got enough milk there for a dozen kids." He squeezed her boob.

Julie winced and slapped his hand away. "Seriously Taz."

"Tell me what you need and I'll get it."

"You want me to make you a list?"

"What's wrong with that?"

"What's wrong with that?" she repeated quietly. It wasn't under her breath or whispered, it was her thinking out loud, trying to figure out the next leg in her argument. She let the water out of the sink. There was a rude sucking sound.

"Don't start pouting."

"I'm not. I'm trying to clear my head." She took a deep breath. "It's kind of insulting. You know. It's like you don't trust me." She felt weird like she was repeating something she'd heard on TV.

"I trust you. I just don't want you touching my money."

Julie laughed more out of frustration than anything else. She gave up then and decided to go check on the laundry when she felt the push. She hit the basement door and sort of collapsed against it. If she wasn't so big and clumsy, she probably would have caught herself. Instead she felt her knees hit the floor.

"Ow."

He helped her up and led her over to the table and she eased into a chair.

"Did you push me?"

He stared at her. She looked in a circle around his head, not wanting to make eye contact. Her heart rate was rising and she deliberately pushed it back.

"I tripped," he said.

She laughed. "And I thought I was the one who was clumsy."

She kept her eyes on her hands, folded on the table in front of her. She heard him shuffle behind her and then his footsteps as he headed back to his man cave.

If she wasn't pregnant, she would have called after him sarcastically, "I'm fine by the way." But that would be stupid considering she moved at sloth speed.

She took a breath and held it for four seconds. Then exhaled.

᷍᷍᷍

If Julie had money, she would have gone to a hotel. So she was glad she didn't because that would give her an excuse to go back the next day. She walked straight into the house.

Nellie was sitting on the couch; Malcolm was on her lap. He smiled at Julie and she smiled back.

"What are you doing out?" Nellie asked.

Julie smiled and shook her head. She moved her purse from one shoulder to the other.

Everett was on the floor putting a piece of furniture together. He grinned up at her. "You're ruining the surprise."

Nellie pointed. "That's your new crib. I know it looks scary right now but Everett should be able to figure it out."

Everett glared at Nellie, "It'll be fine."

"It only cost fifty bucks extra to get the store to assemble it is what I'm saying." Nellie glanced at the door behind Julie, "Taz parking the car?"

"He's at home."

"You came by yourself?"

Julie sat on the chair closest to the door. It was over-stuffed and comfortable. Julie had been with Nellie when she bought it. They were both overwhelmed by the price tag until Nellie said, *Aw, the hell with it.* Julie ran her fingers down the ultra-suede. "Taz pushed me."

"What?"

"He pushed me into a door."

"You mean, he put his hands on you and pushed you?" Nellie made the movements with her hands.

"And then I hit the floor." Julie felt like she was inside of a dream.

"Are you serious?" Everett was getting to his feet.

"Calm down, that's not gonna — "

Everett had already left the room. Nellie's eyes followed him.

"Here." Nellie handed the baby to Julie who balanced him carefully on her baby bump and went after Everett.

Malcolm smiled at Julie. She took his hand and measured it against her own. She'd always had such big hands but Malcolm's were similar to hers. "You're growing so fast," she told him. "Slow down a bit."

She heard the back door open and close. Nellie walked in and looked at her. "Are you hungry?"

Julie shook her head.

"I'll make some popcorn."

Julie stared down at the half-finished crib. It was blue.

ᗤᗤᗤ

Everett sat inside the car. Taz and Julie's house was so big, one of the fanciest houses he'd ever seen. White with a big garage. He remembered breaking into a house like this once. Drank all the booze and passed out on the couch. Even drunk, he didn't feel good enough to sleep in one of its bedrooms.

He glanced at the clock. Ten thirty. By this time, Taz would know she'd left. He'd be starting to get angry before he got scared, so scared that he started thinking of stuff to buy her or cleaned up the kitchen or some other stupid "nice" thing that guys did. Everett had a stepfather once; he knew the drill.

Taz was sitting in the dining room when he walked in. He had a beer in front of him.

"Get up."

"No."

"Get up."

Taz rose to his feet. Everett slammed him in the face. Taz stumbled backwards.

"Fight back."

Taz held his hands in front of him, palms up. "What would be the point?"

It was a fair question, Everett thought, as his second punch connected with Taz's right cheek. A third was a direct hit to his nose. It bled. This made Everett happy. Blood in a fight always had that effect.

Taz held his hands to nose to catch the blood. It was leaking through his fingers. Everett hit him one more time, this time in the gut so he went down to his knees. A rare sight to see a chief on his knees.

Everett pulled out a chair and sat down and reached for a beer.

It took a long time for Taz to get back up. He gave Everett a wary glance as he sat down again. He reached for a towel lying on the table and held it to his nose.

"I thought all your teachings kept you from drinking." His voice was muffled.

Everett took a long sip before answering. "Keeps me from killing you."

He pointed at the forty-inch flat screen staring him in the face. "That new?"

"Yeah."

"We're old married people now. You shouldn't be pulling this shit." Everett's voice sounded weird to him. The room was full of a copper smell. He took another sip of beer. "I've always hated guys like you. Guys who slap around their pregnant girlfriends who can't even fight back."

Taz coughed a bit and spit up what looked like a ball of blood and spit.

"You win. You're the better man." He said, finally. "But I got the bigger TV."

"I'll just get Nellie to buy me one."

Everett picked up a beer and handed it to Taz. "Come on now."

"This is my house." Taz's voice sounded whiny. He must've thought so too because he cleared his throat. "Get the fuck out."

"We're gonna drink up all your booze." Everett looked up at Taz. "And then you're never gonna buy another drop."

Taz stared at Everett like he had a lot to say. But he didn't. Instead he sat down and pulled the beer closer.

Everett took a sip and nodded. "Where's the tunes?"

❧ ❧ ❧

Julie was awake in the guest room. It was in the basement and it was cold down there. She pulled the downy comforter over her head and her world was all white and cozy. She stroked her belly; felt a kick and smiled. "Yes I feel you," she said.

Nellie padded into the room wearing a big thick robe and a long nightdress underneath. Nellie was the only person other than people on TV that Julie had seen wear pyjamas to bed. She sat on the edge of the bed. "How are you feeling?"

"I'm fine." Julie sat up. "It was only a push." She looked down at her hands.

"A push is a push."

"It's never enough though, right?"

"What does that mean?"

"I've left him so many times." Julie wanted to pull the comforter over her head. She felt a cold wind sweep through her body making goosebumps appear on her arms. "I've never made it on my own."

"You have." Julie heard uncertainty in Nellie's voice. She could hear Nellie already organizing Julie's life, putting clothes in dressers and hanging up jackets, calling up friends for favours and finding Julie a sitter, then a job . . .

Julie stared at painting of three Native women silhouetted against the northern lights. One was the mom, one was the child and the third was the grandmother. "The worst time — the time I went away — "

"To Alberta — "

"Yes. He told me it was an accident too. Like he was so drunk that he thought I was someone else and he didn't know what was happening. He told me that in the hospital. He was crying and I felt bad for him. Can you fucking believe that?"

Nellie's eyes were on the clock on the stand next to the bed.

Julie went on, "But it didn't change anything, it didn't make it hurt less, and it didn't bring my baby back."

"The baby?" Nellie's eyes were wide.

Julie continued, wanting to get it all out. "And this time, he was sober so . . . maybe he's getting worse?"

"If I'd known he was hitting you . . . "

"Didn't everyone sort of know?"

Nellie took a deep breath before she nodded. "What kind of person does that make me?"

Julie bowed her head. She wanted to be home, sleeping with her head ten inches from his. Not here, making trouble for people who were trying to be nice to her.

"What kind of person lets someone hurt their child?" Julie's voice was a razor.

Nellie reached for Julie's hand. They weren't touchy-feely the two of them. Julie actually liked that about them. But maybe it was okay to let her friend try to help her. *I am pregnant* she reminded herself. *Like totally knocked up.* Her laugh came out weird. Nellie glanced at her. "You choking?"

Julie shook her head. Nellie took her hand away and rubbed that wrinkle between her eyebrows.

Julie remembered when she used to watch Nellie do her homework. Nellie focussed on every single subject with the same intensity. She would wrap her mind around all of it because it was more important to be good at everything than be great at one thing and suck at a few.

Her voice sounded weird when she spoke. "Would you mind sleeping upstairs? I have to go to the office and pick up my stuff."

Julie shook her head. "You can't leave him too."

But Nellie had already left the room.

At the first glimpse of the sun, Everett rose abruptly from the table and walked out of the room. Taz wasn't surprised to hear the door close behind him. Everett had always been like that. He got a nervous energy when he drank.

Taz stumbled to the bathroom and stared at the tenderized flesh in front of him. Wouldn't be able to hide that at the next meeting. He thought up a good lie and then walked back to the bedroom and fell onto the bed.

A good sleep can fix almost everything his mom used to tell him. "And yet you were never happy," he whispered into his pillow.

The Curtain

April 2008

IT WAS A SMALL room, three chairs padded in a wine-red velvet. Nellie figured it wasn't a real velvet though, some kind of cotton plush product that conference halls used. The rug on the floor looked like it had been stained and cleaned with a tide of carpet cleaners a thousand times. There was a curtain, blue velvet this one, hanging between her and the dull roar of a thousand voices. *Never been on this side before.*

She could feel her intestines twisting in an ancient dance of fear. Her knees shook in time to the beat of her heart. Next her teeth would start chattering and if that happened she was screwed.

I could leave, I could go home. I could say I got sick. But everyone would know I chickened out.

I can do this, Nellie reminded herself. *I've been to law school, I'm a mom, and I've survived a relationship with Everett Kaiswatim — I can handle anything.*

He was out there on the other side, with their son because they still hadn't found a decent sitter.

He didn't know what to make of this, only that if she was sure, then that's all that mattered.

Except I'm not.

The door opened and Taz walked in. He was leaner than he'd been in a long time. She heard through gossip that he went home to Crow's Nest for a bit to sit with the Elders. Nellie knew the truth. He needed to be around his family because Julie still hadn't come home.

"Hey," he said.

"Hi." He looked friendly enough.

"Got your speech ready to go?"

Nellie nodded.

"You look nervous."

She shrugged.

He pulled back the curtain and the roar got louder.

"I never saw a set up like this," he said. "Normally we stand near the stage. This is something fancy. Gives you time to prepare, if you need it."

First strike. Next one would be aimed at her body.

"Nice jeans." He was smirking. "Trying to look like one of the people?"

The jeans had been a calculated choice. She knew her suits weren't going to win anyone over and would in fact alienate most of the crowd who associated dress up clothing with whites and sellouts. And a dress would be weird in this room full of old guys with western shirts tucked into Levis. So jeans it was.

"They're saying you're a lawyer who's never even been to her reserve."

"I grew up on my reserve." *While daydreaming about leaving it forever.* She and Everett had gone home a few weekends before to tell her parents that she was running. Her mom was disappointed; she wanted Nellie to stay home with the baby. Her dad hadn't said anything just raised his eyebrows and asked them if they wanted hotdogs or hamburgers.

"They're calling you an apple."

"I've heard that before." Not to her face but when she heard the description of what an apple was, she knew people would think she fit that mold. Probably the wine-drinking. And the Volvo. But it was such a perfect car. Damn Germans, making her look like a sellout.

"People don't know why you'd want to run."

"Spite."

Taz laughed. "That's the worst reason I've ever heard."

"It's a reason though."

"A shitty one."

"What about yours? Money, power, women? More money?"

"Nobody cares about that. As long as you get things done."

"Did you?"

Taz sighed. "You know I did my best Nellie. They were going to force it down our throats anyway."

Nellie knew this.

"And then you left in the middle of the night like a poor Indian on rent day. Just left me here all alone."

This was true. But . . . "I have my limits Taz. Mine is Julie coming into my house telling me that you hit her."

She saw him flinch. But he didn't turn away. "It'll look good that you're running. Makes ASC look like they're progressive. Few chiefs will even vote for you. Mostly as a *fuck-you* to me.

But nobody wants a woman chief. You're . . . " Taz pretended to check his watch, "about ten years too early."

"Too bad, I'm here now."

"I think you'd make a good leader. But you should start small, like at the reserve level. Y'know learn the ropes."

"You didn't."

"I've been in politics my whole life."

"Seems like you're trying to talk me out of it. Seems like you're scared." Nellie didn't like how she was breathless already.

Taz shrugged. "Not in the least."

A man looked behind the curtain, short and dark with thick glasses, he did the tech for all ASC events. He looked wary of both of them. "You ready?" This was directed at Nellie. She nodded. He dropped the curtain.

Taz tapped her shoulder. "There you go. Knock'em dead."

"I won't. I'm not a good public speaker. My voice is for shit."

"Too bad."

Nellie got up, she smoothed her jeans and pulled the waistband over her leftover belly bump. Damn Native body, her waist so undefined her jeans got confused all the time.

She straightened herself up and looked at Taz who had sat down. She promised Julie that she wouldn't let it happen on stage. She owed him that much. Even now. She owed him for bringing her here. She owed him for a thousand laughs over a table strewn with beer bottles. She owed him for bring her tea. "Taz . . . Julie went to the police."

Taz's jaw tightened. "For what?"

Nellie sighed, her trademark, all-the-way-down-to-her-toes-exhale. "Don't even. You can't be chief with a criminal record. Our rules are tougher than moniyaw rules. You know that."

Nellie picked up her notepad, her bullet points memorized but she wanted it with her anyway.

Never hurt to be prepared. She was still shaking, but shaking Nellie was going to have to be enough.

She looked back up at Taz. He was staring down at his phone. He had a lot of messages.

ক্চ্-ক্চ্-ক্চ্

There was a pain in her lower back like cramps but sharper. Insistent.

Julie was in the living room in the big chair, throwing a ball to Malcolm. He couldn't catch it but he laughed every time it entered the air, bounced on the floor and rolled to his feet.

She had moved in with Nellie and Everett. They were always around her these days. Sheltering her from being one of those women who are single and mothers. But Julie had never felt less alone. Her mom was frequently in her thoughts, offering advice and cautions. Every month they grew closer: *this is where you were at this point, this is how you felt, this is what you were thinking.*

Another ache, this one deeper, like when she was a teenager and would sit against the wall at the school and sometimes a rock would be in your back and you wouldn't bother to move because you were laughing so hard. Where were her friends now? Julie looked around the room. Nellie was working at her computer, her brow wrinkled. Her hair was sprinkled with grey, having no time these days for appointments.

Everett was in the kitchen cooking, the smell wafting in and reminding Julie that she had no appetite. But what about the other ones? Theresa, her favourite smoking friend — Julie heard she moved to Calgary years ago but that was all. Her aunts had not spoken to her since she'd left them in Grande Prairie. She'd even called to tell them about the baby but nobody had picked up. And Shells who Julie thought she saw at a bus stop. But when she called out to her the woman didn't turn around. And Shay was many years gone now but Nellie still flinched when Julie said her name. And Taz, who made Julie freeze in place when she heard his voice. Only last week she stood in the kitchen and shook her head while Nellie offered her the phone. "Julie . . . ? No, she doesn't want to talk. No, I'm not keeping her from you. She's pregnant, idiot. She needs space. . . You take care, too."

Malcolm was creeping. Back to the DVD stand. To pull it down again. Julie reached for him and felt a pain, sharper this time. She breathed through it. Stay in control, that was the advice her doctor gave her. At all times, control your breath. The stand came crashing down, a slick case slid past her foot. Her eyes went to Malcolm, he was free and clear; eyes shining at the drama he had created. Nellie was up and chastising him. "No, no, no. We don't do that." As if he knew what she was saying.

"Julie you feeling okay?"

Julie nodded and leaned back in her chair. She picked up a book and pretended to read it. She would go eventually but she was in no hurry to reach the hospital. The last time she'd been there alone. A nurse fixing the cut above her eye. "Has he hit you there before?" in a voice, slightly bored — *I do this all the time and I am scared of nothing.* Julie refusing to answer because then there would be police. And then the news from a different nurse, "there is no heartbeat." And they both looked away and busied their hands.

Julie felt her own heart pick up speed at the memory. She felt her tummy, felt a movement down there. *Okay, yes, it's okay.*

The pain was there again, like that rock in her back. Outside the high school was where Julie had some of her best times. Listening to the kids joke around and talk about partying like they had forever. They would be out there in all kinds of weather, the roof shielding them from rain, the three sides protecting them from most winds, only the coldest days driving them inside. They'd try though, they would huddle together in their leather jackets and thin coats and laugh into the circle, their smoke thick and slow in the cold air.

Inside was where futures were and they had none, no matter how much the nice teachers tried to tell them it was there for them too. Better to smoke and laugh than hope for anything else. Better to enjoy that brief time they got to be together.

There was a deer one time. Julie and one of her friends were outside getting stoned on the thinnest joint the world had ever seen. Julie saw the deer in the woods moving in and out of the trees. Flashes of brown. That slender head pointed at them, those dark eyes watching them. Julie stared back, wished she knew a call to bring her closer. Tell her it was safe.

Another cramp, this one enough to make her clench her teeth. *Breathe. Breathe. Breathe.*

"We will have to go soon."

"But not — yet."